'Winnette's Western world still resonates with the
trope-filled works of the genre's greats'
— *Heavy Feather Reviews*

'Great book [that helped prove] 2015 Was the Year
the Literary Versus Genre War Ended'
— *Vice*

'One of those novels that challenges you to find a good
moment to put it down' — *Midnight Breakfast*

'Kind of refreshing, bizarre, remorseless story the Western
genre needs' — *Ask Men*

'Raw and cut throat and still capable of reducing you
to helpless snickers'
— *Full Stop*

'The novel is both haunting and haunted'
— *The Oyster Review*

'Dark, riveting drama'
— *Alibi*

'Striking and powerful'
— *Electric Literature*

'A journey into a hallucinatory West'
— *Vol. 1 Brooklyn*

'Packed with action'
— *Cultured Vultures*

Also by Colin Winnette

CRITICAL ACCLAIM FOR *HAINTS STAY*

'In his astonishing portrait of American violence,
Haints Stay, Colin Winnette makes use of the Western
genre to stunning effect'
– *LA Times*

'*Haints Stay* turns the Western on its ear' – *Washington Post*

'*Haints Stay* puts to mind the very best contemporary
novels of the old West... But Colin Winnette has his own
dark and delightful and surprising agenda. Be wary. He
might be the new law in town'
– Sam Lipsyte, author of *The Fun Parts* and *The Ask*

'Winnette portrays his serial killers with an odd grace
and punctuates his circular narrative with murders, revenge killings,
a shooting spree, and a heroic arc for wannabe gunslinger Bird that
is broadly, darkly humorous'
– *Kirkus Reviews*

'Funny, brutal and haunting, *Haints Stay* takes the
traditional Western, turns it inside out, eviscerates it,
skins it, and then wears it as a duster...'
– Brian Evenson, author of *The Open Curtain*

'I loved it. Loved it! *Haints Stay* had me from the very first
line – the visceral ante upped and crescendoing nearly
every page. Humor, gore, that wonderful unsettling feeling
you get when you're reading a book that excites you and
kind of scares you as well? Yes, please'
– Lindsay Hunter, author of *Ugly Girls* and *Don't Kiss Me*

'[One of the] 50 Best Independent Press Books of 2015'
— *Flavor Wire*

'[One of] LitReactor's favorite reads of 2015'
— *Lit Reactor*

'[One of their] Favourite novels of 2015'
— *Large Hearted Boy*

'Read it soon' — *Fourth and Sycamore*

'[One of the best] Overlooked Books of 2015'
— *Slate*

'A gritty, modern acid western'
— *Book Riot*

'Winnette gives his characters fascinating depth and masterfully
pushes the novel far outside the genre's boundaries'
— *River City Reading*

'Damn good read' — *Numero Cinq*

'From dialogue to action, Winnette does many things
right in this novel'
— *The Collagist*

'The cinematic quality to this work is undeniable'
— *Portland Mercury*

HAINTS STAY

COLIN WINNETTE

NO EXIT PRESS

647252

First published in the UK in 2016 by No Exit Press,
an imprint of Oldcastle Books Ltd,
PO Box 394, Harpenden,
Herts, AL5 1XJ, UK
noexit.co.uk
@noexitpress

A CIP catalogue record for this book is available from the British Library.

ISBN
978-1-84344-834-1 (Print)
978-1-84344-845-8 (Epub)
978-1-84344-836-5 (Kindle)
978-1-84344-837-2 (Pdf)

2 4 6 8 10 9 7 5 3 1

Typeset by Avocet Typeset, Somerton, Somerset
Printed in Great Britain by Clays Ltd, St Ives plc

This book is for bug

BROOKE AND SUGAR WERE ON A BRIDGE

between a field and a crowded wood. They had lost their horses days ago and had been walking for miles on end. The bridge was where they decided to break. Out in the open. A kind of celebration.

Sugar unpacked a few slices of bread and a brick of old cheese. He tore chunks loose with his nails and set them on the open face of the bread at his side. Brooke spat between his knees and took pleasure in the smacking sound as his saliva met the water below.

They had finished a job. They were emptied of bullets and powder. They were satisfied men. They were on their way to collect the next few months' security. To be cleaned and taken care of. They would be treated well again, their shoulders and their genitals rubbed. They would smoke and bathe at the same time. Sugar would buy dinners and drinks and comb his hair with scented oils. Brooke would gamble and win and lose, but no one would be after him. He would buy a new knife. They were victorious and cheerful as ever they could be.

It was another day or two before they reached the town. They camped out in the open, unsheltered. Sugar smoked on his back with a strip of fabric covering his eyes. Each night, Brooke counted the stars until he fell asleep and woke blinded by the one.

✝ ✝ ✝

As they neared the town, they smelled smoke. Not the welcoming kind, the tin-chimney and clay-pot kind, but an acrid, overwhelming kind of smoke. They continued. It was only a few minutes before they noticed the thin gray funnels rising up and opening out to the clouds above them.

In essence the town remained, but its landscape had changed. Jenny's had been razed. People moved past the bar as if it were nothing to see at all. And there wasn't much. What remained of the walls was blackened and halved. A streaked set of spiraling stairs near the center of the lot wound upward to nothing. The pole at the banister's base supported the charred head of an eagle.

The bathhouse stood fine as it ever had, only a man now hunched at the doorway. They didn't know him. He had the clean, fat look of an out-of-towner. He wore a thin-brimmed hat and a charcoal vest.

"I'm Brooke," said Brooke, "and this is my brother Sugar."

Sugar nodded, put out his hand.

The clean, fat stranger nodded and opened the door to them.

Sugar lowered his hand, slid it into his pocket. They were used to disrespect. They did not take it personally.

Brooke followed his brother into the lobby of the bathhouse. It was cleaner than usual and bustling. They positioned themselves in line behind an elderly man hunched against a thin cane. He smiled at them and Sugar smiled brightly back.

"Good afternoon," he said. "Was there an accident at the bar?"

The elderly man shook his head. He stuck out a nub where his tongue should have been. He turned from them and arranged himself against the cane again.

Sugar tapped Brooke's elbow, stuck out his tongue, and point-ed at what the elderly man had been missing. Brooke nodded. He saw what Sugar saw, just the same as Sugar saw it, but Sugar insisted on telling it back to him.

"You're the two boys without a father," said a very thin man, suddenly at their side. He too wore a vest and a thin-brimmed hat.

They nodded. It was how people chose to see them. The truth was they had plenty of fathers, but that wasn't what people meant when they said *father*. They had that kind of father too, the kind that gave Sugar his thick hair and Brooke his crooked nose. There was a single man responsible for the husks of both brothers, only no one knew which man he was or had been and Brooke and Sugar did not care for them to.

"Come with me, then," said the man at their side.

They followed. With the bar gone and their payment delayed, at the very least, they were willing to investigate whatever new opportunities were presented them. Things changed in town. They changed often. There was no use fighting it. What they did was, they found a way and worked it until they found a new one.

They were seated before an oak desk and the tiny man behind it.

"You see the bar?" said the tiny man. "Do you know who burned it?"

Brooke and Sugar watched the tiny man smile and lean back in his desk chair.

"Me," said the tiny man, "and the women inside and the men inside. *Your* man inside. Your woman inside."

The tiny man pointed at Sugar. He had soft eyes, the tiny man behind the desk. Soft and black, like pencil lead.

11

Sugar shifted in his seat. He brought a strip of fabric out from the front pocket of his tattered suit and wiped his brow theatrically. A signal to the man that he meant no harm, that he was willing to appear intimidated. It wasn't their show, and they knew it.

Brooke examined the desk: a jar of pens, an ivory letter opener atop a stack of papers, an ashtray containing one smoldering cigarillo.

"You think I've got ideas I don't," said the tiny man. "I know this won't stick. I'm not here to stay. I'm a link in a chain of things I've got no idea how to stop or predict."

He barely occupied his chair. He was like a cat in the lap of a giant. He was sweating too, and Sugar thought to pass the fabric to him in a gesture of brotherly goodwill.

"But I'm here for now," said the tiny man. "And you're the first problem I can see coming."

"Because we're owed by the bar," said Brooke.

"There isn't a bar," said the tiny man. "Not anymore." He laughed and tilted back in his chair and laughed some more, his hand at his belly. Darkness and rot freckled the inside of his mouth. His teeth and gums were lit by the room's light as he laughed and held his mouth open like an offering.

Sugar smiled. Brooke examined a nearby shelf, the spines of the books there and the dust that had long ago settled on them. The dust of another man's body, another man's toil and time.

After a moment the tiny man regained his composure and opened the drawer to his left. He slid the letter opener from the exposed desktop down into the drawer.

"Money," said the tiny man, "or some other thing that will make you resentful of the bar going down. Maybe you two like to drink. Maybe you two like women. Maybe you're sentimental.

12

I can't have two thorns wandering the streets, looking for a reason to stick in my side."

The tiny man seemed to relax then.

"So," he said, settling back into the enormous-looking chair and letting his thin arms dangle from either side, "how can I trust you two to keep your heads about you?"

"Do you read history?" said Sugar.

"Yes and no," said the tiny man, a smile creeping back into his lips. "I don't read much, but I know a few things. History, as you put it, it's slippery."

"Well I'm a student of history," said Sugar, "and any observant man can see that power is like a gold coin. Some men squander it, throw it away on nothing worth noticing. Others simply lose it to a world that's much hungrier for it than they are. Others still dedicate their lives to holding onto it. And some die, coin in hand, surrendering it only to the men who bury them."

The tiny man inched forward in his seat, eyed Sugar for a point.

"My brother and I," said Sugar, "it makes no difference to us what the world does with its money."

"You're too... uh, historically read, huh," said the tiny man, "to get hung up on something like an unpaid debt? Or an ignorant, rot-mouthed cunt taking the reins?"

"No," said Brooke, "but we'd settle for a modest homecoming of sorts. We'd like a bath each. We'd like the promise of a bed or two with a window, at least temporarily. The peace of mind to rest. We've been traveling for days. We lost our beloved horses with many miles still between us and here. Give us the opportunity to get fresh, to adjust. We'll keep our pampered heads about us."

Sugar placed the fabric back into his front pocket. He crossed his legs and eyed the tiny man, who looked at Brooke as if he were still speaking. Finally, the tiny man nodded and a hand set itself on Brooke's shoulder.

Brooke had the ashtray from the desk in his hand then and was already withdrawing the blow he'd spent on the broken-nosed thug behind him. Blood spilled from the thug's nose. He clutched his face as if trying to collect the blood that gathered there.

Brooke set the ashtray back on the desk and Sugar settled himself into his chair.

"Okay," said the tiny man, with a grin. "A bath it is."

The baths were crowded. Men of indeterminate age, but none of them young, lined the edges. A mix of tobacco smoke and steam crowded the air. Sagging wooden guardrails led down a row of steps into the water of the communal bath. The floor and walls wore a yellowing tile.

The heat pressed against Brooke's and Sugar's lungs as they moved along the bath's perimeter to hang their towels from a row of silver hooks lining the far wall.

Someone whistled. Others coughed, shifted, and began to whisper.

"I think they like you," said Brooke.

Sugar smiled and Brooke stepped into the water. The blood on his left hand lifted and dispersed. He bent at the knees and submerged himself up to his shoulders. He shut his eyes, listened to the sounds of the other men as they examined his brother.

"You don't even smell like a woman," said a longhaired man sitting alone in the corner of the large square, now shared by nearly twenty men.

14

Sugar had seated himself on the bench lining the edge of the bath. He crossed his legs, then thought again and uncrossed them. He parted his knees just slightly. He nodded at the long-haired man sitting a foot or so from him.

"It's because I'm not a woman," said Sugar. He snapped his fingers at a passing boy in white. The boy paused and removed a thin cigarette from a pack on the silver tray he carried before him. Sugar gripped it with his lip and the boy lit it with a smile.

"Your charge number, sir?"

"It's on your man," said Sugar, and the boy nodded. He made a mark in a small notebook beside the cigarette pack on the tray and began again to circle the bath's perimeter.

"You've got the finer parts," said the longhaired man. "I don't mean at all to pry or stare. I just haven't seen a woman's parts… in years, and… well you don't expect to come across them in a place like this."

"Is he bothering you, Sugar?" Brooke rose from the water before them. He was lean and cruel looking. He looked as if he should have been covered in scars, but all of the wounds he bore were fresh. His muscles were mottled with age and effort.

"No," said Sugar. He let the smoke drift between his vaguely parted lips. "He's just admiring my parts."

The longhaired man smiled and shifted and put his hands up. "No," he said, "I'm just noticing is all. I don't mean either of you any discomfort or trouble." He slunk away to a far corner of the bath and settled between two older men who were lean-ing against the bath's edge, eyes closed, either sleeping or dead.

Brooke took his spot there in the corner near his brother.

"You should cross your knees," he said. "In a place like this."

"You should avoid giving advice," said Sugar. "You haven't got the face for it."

"Did you notice our friend?" said Brooke. He ran his palms along the surface of the water, examined the edges of his scabs as they softened.

"How long do you think we've got?" said Sugar.

"Get your hair wet," said Brooke. "Then we should go."

The broke-nosed thug was bleeding between two gangly men in the bath adjacent to Brooke and Sugar. His eyes had not lifted from their movements.

Sugar crab-walked out from the bench and lowered himself under the water. He ran his hands back and forth through his hair and could feel the grit coming away in sleeves. He opened his eyes to see the water had yellowed around him. He picked at the pieces that clung directly to his scalp. He felt a shiver in his shoulders, the rare delight of a long-awaited bath. He admired his brother's legs through the chalky water. The pressure in Sugar's lungs grew more intense with each passing moment. He exhaled and Brooke's legs lifted suddenly up and out of the bath. Sugar kicked himself toward the far edge of the bath and rose up and out as well.

Brooke was on top of the naked, broke-nosed thug, pounding his chest and stomach and face. The sound was that of a cow collapsing into mud, again and again and again.

Brooke broke the skin of the broke-nosed thug in various patches about his body. Brooke rose only when the reach of the blood surpassed his wrists. He rose naked and bloody and examined the room. Some looked angry, put out. Others were frightened and without a plan. The longhaired man who had been talking to Sugar sank between the two old men at either side of him, until the water reached his ears. He eyed the brothers across the surface of the water, bubbling air from his slender nose.

16

Sugar gathered their towels from the hooks and Brooke backed slowly into his as Sugar opened it to greet him.

They left the bath together, dressed hurriedly in the adjoining room where they had left their clothes, and sped toward the front door with the air of practiced men.

They were back in the woods only a few minutes later. They had slid out of town, uninterrupted. It wasn't a hard thing to do, to disappear when they needed to. It just wasn't what they'd been hoping for.

"I can't do another night of this," said Sugar. He was standing, pacing, looking between the trees.

"At least we got the bath." Brooke set his head on a small rock at the base of a tree. It was sundown. The woods were cooling around them.

No one was after them. They'd been given no chase. They were gone and that was all that mattered. In a place like that, in a time like this, people had more immediate concerns. All the better if he'd killed the pummeled thug. He was the only one who might have taken the whole thing personally.

"Have we got another plan?" said Sugar.

Brooke set his hands palm down where his ribs met his belly. "Perhaps we'll live and die in the woods," he said.

Finally, Sugar sat. The night grew dark. They talked on as their eyes adjusted. They got along well when there were empty hours ahead. They'd been out for so long already, it was almost easier for them to talk like they still were, like they'd never been back. Only things were soured now. They hadn't the same tolerance they'd had when headed home.

17

"We'll just wait a few days," said Brooke. "No one's going to care in a week."

"So we'll wait a week, or a few days?" said Sugar.

"We'll just wait," said Brooke, "until it feels right."

"Here's what's eating me," said Sugar. "The man you nearly killed. What was he hoping to get out of approaching us in the bath?"

"What do you mean?" Brooke rolled on to his side to examine his bedded-down brother.

"I mean, was he after you for breaking his nose, or to finish what he'd started?"

"The difference being?"

"The difference being, one agenda is personal. The other was a task assigned him by the same tiny man who sent us to enjoy his newly acquired facilities, only moments after you broke the nose of a man in his employ."

"Okay," said Brooke, "it's a question that warrants asking. And yet I don't think the answer makes much of a difference. Either way we'll be in the woods tonight. We'll listen for the approach of a man, and if we don't hear it, we'll wait a day or two and then go home. We'll find a bed and a private shower. We'll stay out of anyone's hair until they need us or come looking."

"And what if they no longer need us?"

"We've never been without work."

"Times are lean. You saw the people back there. Not a lot of children. Not a lot of fat."

"You've got a quality perceptive mind, Sugar. I could listen to you for days on end."

"What purpose do killers serve in a town that's already dying?"

"And poetic too."

"People aren't living like they used to, Brooke." Sugar sat up to face his brother.

"They never have," said Brooke. Then, "The door man."

"The door man," said Sugar.

"He was fat."

"He was muscular, maybe, but…"

"No, fat. He was fat, Sugar."

"Okay. And he was in the tiny man's employ. So he's keeping the town slim and fattening up his men. An army of giants to protect a child."

"I miss Henry."

"We'll find a new Henry."

"Henry was special."

"Henry was a horse."

"He was a special horse, Sugar."

"You're the only one who lost a horse?"

"I miss Buck too."

"Well, I miss Buck and Henry too."

They were silent then. Sugar tilted his body as if to suggest he was listening for the broke-nosed thug. Brooke opened his eyes and stared into the brilliant dark. He pressed his fingers into the dirt on either side of him and felt the stones and teeth buried there.

"How old are we, Brooke?"

"Why would I know that?"

"You seem to know so much about our life and how we should live it. I thought you could answer one honest question."

"We'll get two new horses. They will be stronger and livelier than the old ones."

"Henry and Buck."

"Than Henry and Buck, yes, and they'll serve us well and

we'll love them as we loved Henry and Buck, and then they'll die and we'll get more horses. And on and on, Sugar. Now sleep."

Brooke's hand was occupied by a foreign object. He felt it before opening his eyes to greet the day, which had rose up around them like a warm fog. Here they were, back in the woods again and holding one another as they had always done on cold nights. But Sugar felt different to him that morning. Smaller, thinner. Cleaner. Brooke felt a bone protruding, sharper than those he knew to be Sugar's. He spoke a few casual sounds and received no answer and opened his eyes to reveal a young boy, hardly a hair on his body, sleeping between Brooke and his brother as heavily as a dead horse.

"Sugar."

His brother did not stir.

"Sugar, there's a boy here."

Sugar rolled slightly but did not rise.

"Sugar," said Brooke, and this time the boy was rocked casually in place before opening his eyes to discover the two men at his flank.

"Who are you?" said the boy.

"I'd like to ask the same question, and add a 'How did you get here and between us?'" said Brooke. He rose and dusted himself, examined the woods around them for a set of eyes or ears or a broken nose. The woods were silent but for the small birds plunging into the pine needles gathered at the base of each enormous tree. They were utterly alone, the two brothers and their stranger.

"I don't know," said the boy. He said it plainly and without fright. He seemed as comfortable as the leaves around them.

"You don't know which?" said Brooke. He kicked Sugar, finally, to wake him.

"It's horse shit," said Sugar, unsteadily, his eyes still shut.

"It's an escape," said Brooke. "You're hiding out?"

Again, the boy said, "I don't know."

"Well," said Sugar, "who are you?" He was up finally, watching the boy, puzzling out how slow he might actually be, or how capable a liar.

"Who are you?" said the boy. He put his hands to his face, rubbed, coughed. He brought his hands down and examined the two men. "You're going to hurt me?"

"Let's assume no one is going to hurt anyone," said Brooke. "I'm Brooke. This is my brother Sugar. We're killers by trade and we're hiding in the woods after a rout of sorts."

"You're…"

"Killers," said Sugar, "hiding out." He was waking up, pacing again and looking between the trees.

The boy seemed weak, a little slow. Incapable of harm, or at least uninterested.

"Who… who did you kill?"

"Which time?" said Sugar.

"Stop it, Sugar." Brooke poured something black from a leather pouch into a tin cup. He handed it to the boy, "My brother is trying to scare you."

"Why?" asked the boy.

"Because you're wrong not to be frightened of two men sleeping in the woods," said Sugar. "Especially these two men."

"When you say you don't know where you came from or who you are," said Brooke, "what exactly do you mean? Where were you yesterday? Where were you an hour ago?"

"I don't know."

21

"Everyone comes from somewhere," said Sugar. "Where are your clothes? What have you got in your pockets?"

"I don't have anything," said the boy. He was nude and empty-handed. There was nothing in the piles about them that did not belong to Sugar and Brooke, that they had not bedded down with the night before. The boy had nothing to him but his person.

"There's meat on your bones," said Sugar. He cracked the bones in his fingers, one by one, then his neck and back. He rose and stood before the boy. "You've eaten recently enough. You don't look ill or wounded."

The boy nodded slowly. "I don't feel ill or wounded."

"Hm," said Sugar. He leaned forward slightly and set his hand to his waist. He turned and walked into the woods around them and after a few moments his figure disappeared into the mist. They could hear him crushing leaves and cracking twigs with his boots. They could hear faintly the sound of his breathing.

"What's he doing?" said the boy. "Where's he gone?"

"Don't mind it," said Brooke.

"Are you going to hurt me?"

"I don't think so," said Brooke. "If you tell us why you're here. If you can tell us why we shouldn't. You can tell the truth, boy. Are you a scout? A young gunslinger trying an impoverished angle? Did you grow up on a perfectly normal farm with perfectly simple parents who were very casual people and did not bother much with towns or neighbors? Were you looking to get out and see the world? Or did your people torture you and send you running into the night?"

"I haven't done anything," said the boy. He was crying without whimpering or whining, letting the tears roll from the corners of his eyes in crooked lines down to his mouth. "What's he doing?"

"Don't worry about him," said Brooke.

"Where's he gone?"

"He's ill," said Brooke. "We're not doctors. We don't like them. It will stop eventually."

"I don't understand."

"Neither do I. He's my brother. It's always been this way."

"What's your name?"

"Brooke. Now yours."

The boy examined his palms.

"I don't know," said the boy. "I don't know anything."

"Where were you before?"

"I don't know."

"What do you remember?"

"What do you mean?"

"What do you remember about where you were before? What do you picture in your head when you think about elsewhere?"

"I picture you and... Sugar?"

"Sugar."

"You and Sugar. That's all I know. And some voices."

"What are they saying?"

"I can't tell. It's just sounds. From a distance."

"You don't remember anything else?"

The boy shook his head.

"Your mother? Your father? What you had for breakfast yesterday?"

The boy was silent a moment. He examined his palms.

"Can I... can I see your hands?" said the boy.

"Where are these words coming from then? What you're saying? Who taught you to speak and speak like us?"

The boy shrugged. He was crying again.

Brooke put out his palms. They were caked in dirt, a little blood in the deeper wrinkles, which had run from a small crack in the skin between his knuckles. The boy slid his hands under his legs, palms down and pressing into the dirt.

Sugar approached.

"What'd you get?" said Brooke.

"What business is it of yours?"

"Are you sick?" said the boy.

"No," said Sugar.

"Are you hurt?"

"You're a curious little egg, aren't you? We're done with this. You need to get along anyhow. Back to nowhere."

"Sugar," said Brooke.

"And if someone comes looking for us tonight, tomorrow, or any day after this, for that matter," Sugar leaned in, "we're going to know where he came from. Whether or not you actually said something, we've got to act on what we know, pursue reason and statistical likelihood above all else—so we're going to find you and the people who matter most to you. Did we explain what it is we do for a living, son? Did we make it clear enough? We'll go right to work on you, and anyone who knows your name."

"Sugar," said Brooke.

"We'll erase you. Any trace of you."

"Sugar," said Brooke.

The boy was crying openly, his palms still buried beneath his thighs. He was flexing his fingers and digging into the leaves beneath him, loosing small rocks and the end of a buried twig.

"I'm telling the truth," said Sugar.

"You've scared him, Sugar. Now leave him alone," said Brooke.

Finally the boy brought his hands to his face, tried to turn away from them. Sugar snapped him up by the wrists and held out his arms as if the boy were pleading. The boy stared up at him but said nothing.

"Sugar, let him go," said Brooke, and Sugar held out the boy's palms to Brooke and pointed with his chin. The palms were blank, staring back at them. Smooth as stones.

"Have you ever caught anything before?" said Brooke.

The boy was on his belly at Brooke's side and they were watching two deer hoof their way crosswise up a steep and sudden incline only a mile or so from where the men had been camped that morning.

"I don't know," said the boy.

"Let's say you haven't," said Brooke. "You're going to feel a certain kind of pride, a sense of accomplishment. But you're also going to feel uneasy with that, as if there's something wrong with it. There isn't. It's as natural as breathing. That guilt is all fear, anyway. Fear that one day you're going to be on the receiving end of a blow, and the sudden wish that no one had to do that kind of thing ever. You can rid yourself of all that if you just accept what's coming to you in the general sense, and work to prevent it in the immediate sense. No matter what you let live you're going to die and it's just as likely it will be of a rock falling on your head or getting a bad cough as it is that someone will decide they want you gone. So accept it now and move on."

"Okay," said the boy.

"Are you ready?" said Brooke.

"I think so," said the boy.

"We'll wait then," said Brooke.

The deer worked their way up the steep incline without struggle. As they neared the top, the boy said, "I don't think your brother likes me."

"He doesn't trust you," said Brooke.

"Why?"

"He's no reason to."

"Okay," said the boy.

Brooke watched him a moment. Then the boy said, "I'm ready," and they rose up and loosed their stones from their slings.

The boy missed entirely, but Brooke's stone made contact with the larger of the two and when the creature stumbled, stunned, a few feet down the incline, Brooke took off. He collapsed onto the stunned animal, gripped its jaw, its shoulder, twisted and snapped some hidden, necessary part. Everything about the deer went still, then it kicked, shuddered, and went still again.

"We'll eat," said Brooke.

"I won't eat it," said the boy.

Brooke was sawing the skin from the kill, its legs spread and tied to two separate trees. Brooke shrugged and placed the knife beneath a long length of flesh.

"Then you'll die," said Brooke.

✝   ✝   ✝

That night they heard men on the road. Voices in the dark. The boy woke first. He trembled and rubbed his body beneath the shirt Brooke had given him, which the boy hadn't put on, but chose instead to lay over himself as a blanket.

He heard laughter from several men and a single struggling voice. Grunting and squealing just a little, breathing in spurts.

"I think someone's found us," said the boy.

Brooke and Sugar did not stir.

"Brooke," said the boy. "Sugar. I think someone's—"

And Brooke was up. He was quiet, moving, sifting through his bag. His hand withdrew clutching a piece of metal that shone silver in the moonlight. Brooke disappeared then, into the trees. Sugar, the boy suddenly noticed, had vanished too.

As the voices approached, the boy scrambled toward a large dark tree and crouched down on the side opposite their apparent approach.

A limping body scrambled into their campsite, knocking their empty cans with its feet and tripping into the bundles of their supplies. It struggled to lift itself with two skinny arms but four men were suddenly upon it. They dragged it from amongst the supplies and blankets, out to an open spot of grass, faintly lit from the light above. There, they proceeded to kick and strike at the body without a word between them. One stepped back to grab a slick bundle of deer meat from the food pile and bring it down upon the struggling body with something like a laugh, cough, or wheeze. The bundle burst and the boy could hear the meat spilling out and into the grass, then their kicking and stepping on it as they moved about.

"It's meat," said a voice.

"Did we kill him?" said another.

"It's animal meat," said a third.

"Is he dead then?"

The body was no longer struggling, but the boy could make out the chest's movement from several feet away. It breathed like a man asleep, long, deep breaths punctuated by only a moment of stillness.

"He's not dead."

"It's a campsite."

"Who's here?"

"No one."

"The blankets are warm."

One man held Sugar's blanket to his face, smelling and then rubbing it against his cheeks.

"It's a woman," he said.

"Let me," said another voice, grabbing the blanket and pressing it to his face.

"Where is she?"

"Got to be near."

The beaten man began to rise again, lifting himself on two skinny arms then pushing off from the dirt and setting out to run while bent at the waist, clutching his gut as the loose bits of deer fell from him and back into the grass.

"He's up," said a voice, and pursued him.

The one holding the blanket wrapped it around his waist and tied a knot.

"It's mine," said a voice.

"Get after him," said the one with the blanket, and within moments, they set upon their pursued.

They had him down again, pressed against the earth. This time, a knife was drawn. One of the shadows set to sawing at the howling body, and it writhed for a moment before settling back into the ground like a dark, dull piece of landscape.

The boy was shivering, watching them remove pieces of their kill and set them in what must have been pockets or pouches he could not see. They disassembled their kill, much like Brooke had disassembled the deer—hungrily, without hesitation, but with pride.

"Gather what food they have and whatever else is useful," said a voice. "Count the blankets."

The three other men set upon the camp while their apparent commander continued to saw at the body before him.

"Two blankets," said a voice, "and tamped down earth evidencing a third body somewhere."

"Warm?"

"All warm."

"Women?"

"One woman and something small."

"A child."

"A family."

"They're hiding then. Still here somewhere."

"Are you still here?" The voice was yelling, turning its way through the darkness.

Something within the boy wanted to cry out. He curled his lips inward and held them together with his teeth. Something was working its way up and out of him. He felt out of control and desperate, as if he were about to die. If he made a sound, they would be upon him. If they stepped any more in his direction, they would feel his presence and be upon him. If they discovered him, no one would save him.

"Hey," yelled the voice. "You."

"Set their things into a pile and burn them. If they're on the run, whatever it is they're running from will appreciate the help."

The three men gathered Brooke and Sugar's belongings into a pile. Onto the pile they poured something that occupied the boy's nostrils and brought water to his eyes. The pile took flame and two of the men grabbed the carcass of their mutilated catch and dragged it behind the two other men, who were now making haste before them.

Brooke and Sugar's few belongings burned, and the boy released into a small pile at the base of the tree behind which he had been hiding. He breathed and breathed and breathed again, imagining the four men appearing suddenly again and gripping him by the hair and dragging him out, out into the darkness where he would vanish completely and be no more.

Brooke and Sugar appeared then at his side and Sugar lifted him. They moved from the rough fire spilling out onto the grass and crackling throughout the woods. They walked and the boy shook. Soon the woods were blue with the oncoming sun and they were in a landscape that looked no different than what had come before, other than its absence of fire, its relative quiet and the new light born from between the branches of the trees.

"They took our food," said Brooke.

"They were locusts," said Sugar.

"Are they coming back?" said the boy.

"Not on purpose, I imagine," said Sugar.

"I'd like to kill them," said Brooke. "I'd like our things back."

"Our things are gone," said Sugar. "We'll acquire new things."

"Not our deer," said Brooke.

"Our deer is gone," said Sugar.

"They've got our bundles," said Brooke.

"Why did you hide?" said the boy.

"Why did you?" said Sugar.

"We didn't hide," said Brooke. "We waited and watched."

"Were those men after you?" said the boy.

"No," said Sugar. "They were after something else. But now they know we're out here."

"And they've got our deer," said Brooke.

"Will you not be able to let this go?" said Sugar.

"I don't think so," said Brooke. "I'd like to eat. I'd like to avenge our blankets."

"Then we'll return to the site and follow their trail until we overtake them," said Sugar.

The smell of the fire was still thick in the air. Its source, easy to locate. The ashes were wet—drowned hastily with water or urine—but still smoldering beneath a cool layer. Dew spattered the trampled grass. A bent streak of grass, mud, and blood led out into the woods.

"They're very long gone if they're any kind of travelers," said Sugar.

"We're traveling light," said Brooke, "compared."

They poked into the ashes with a branch each and upturned nothing of use.

The boy was shivering, wet with sweat and dew.

Sugar handed him a pinch of tobacco from his sock and the boy put it in his mouth.

"You smoke it," said Sugar, a thin sticky paper pinched between his thumb and pointer finger.

The boy spat out the threads and scraped at his tongue with his fingernails. Sugar put away the paper.

Brooke followed the edge of where a body had fallen and

then been dragged into the woods. The streak wound its way through the trees for as far as his eyes could see. Sugar followed close behind, and then the boy, still scraping at his tongue with his dirty nails.

They heard the four men before they saw them. The boy clung involuntarily to Sugar. The men had taken no precaution to go unseen. They were all laughter and campfire in a clearing. It was barely dusk, nearly nighttime. Brooke and Sugar did not speak, but separated to trace a half circle, several feet from the men and their fire. The boy clung to Sugar for several feet before Sugar paused, gripped the boy's two hands, and pulled them from his own shirt, detaching him. He kept one small hand cupped in each of his own. He led the boy by those two small hands to a tall, wide tree and sat him on its opposite side. Sugar raised a finger to his lips then released his grip, abandoning the boy to watch the woods opening out and away from what was about to happen. As Sugar retreated to his post, the boy watched the open wood for only a moment before shifting to the tree's edge and following Sugar's movements with his gaze.

The boy could not tell for sure, but the four men seemed suddenly hesitant, maybe even alarmed. They quieted. They glanced about themselves. One held a knife in his left hand. It had a thin curving blade. Suddenly Brooke and Sugar were upon them, and Brooke had sunk his thumbs into the eyes of the one with the blade. He collected the blade and stepped away from the flailing body. Sugar was sawing through the rigid meat of another man's gut with a tool the boy could not make out from where he sat. Brooke took the curving blade then and applied it to the neck of yet another man, opening him up like a coin purse and spilling his contents onto the blankets and bundles before him. The fourth man rose and made for Sugar, who turned to receive the first blow. He was knocked into the coals of the fire and Brooke came up behind the fourth man and set at slicing him in the lower ribs and back with the curving blade, over and again. The man had something horrible about him that did not moan or stutter at the cuts. Instead he turned to greet the knife with his open palm, to accept it as if it were an offering. The blade remained in his palm as he drew it from Brooke's grip. He held the pierced palm up over his crooked face, and unsheathed the blade from the net of bone and flesh.

Sugar had batted the coals and ash from his body and was collected then, lunging toward the man holding the knife and approaching Brooke. The man swung around and greeted Sugar's advance. Back and forth he swung to counter the movements of Brooke and Sugar, who were slowly gaining inches on him. The man then threw the curving knife with enough force to puncture Brooke's advancing thigh, and as Sugar leapt toward him from behind, he dodged the advance and moved forward to recollect the knife from Brooke's leg. Brooke howled for only a moment, then watched as the man moved away to make a safe distance between the three of them. There was blood at his mouth. Even more at his ear. He was staggering now, soaked in blood down the back of his shirt and pants. He appeared light and trembling. Brooke and Sugar watched him like a wounded deer. He was nearly set to bleed out and they would have him. They waited and the boy watched and the fourth man glanced around the campsite to confirm that he had lost each and every one of his men. There were bloody piles and bundles gathered by the bedding. A low fire. The woods were quiet until the man dropped to his knees. He held the knife out with both hands now, a bit of slobber at his chin.

"There will only be more men like us," he said. He coughed and spat. "You will only kill and kill until you are overcome."

Brooke stepped forward as if to offer himself up to the man.

"Would you like to stick me one last time before we finish you?" he said. He set his good leg out before their kill. He leaned back to smile at Sugar, who shook his head and plucked tobacco from his sock.

"Don't be grotesque," said Sugar, as the man plunged the curving knife into the bones of Brooke's foot.

The boy came finally from behind the tree as they were gathering up the four men's belongings and placing them in the center of the clearing. They had leaned the bodies against the surrounding trees and the men sat slumped as if napping, their chins to their chests, their palms at their sides, opening skyward.

"Meat," said Brooke, cinching then letting fall one of the bundles.

"Probably their man's," said Sugar.

"Probably our deer's," said Brooke. He plucked a separate bundle from the stack and held it to his nose. "Or neither," he said. "This one isn't fresh."

"Who... who were they?" said the boy.

Brooke slid the curving knife out of his belt and held it out.

"Take their teeth," he said. He held out a small bag. "Place them in here."

"Why?" said the boy.

"So we can bury them with their ghosts," said Brooke.

"I don't know how."

The boy would not take the bag or knife. He clasped his hands behind his back and watched Brooke's face as he explained there was no particular way to do it, just saw into the gums until the teeth came loose in your hand.

"There will be blood, but not more than you can handle. And remember," he explained, "they can't feel it."

"Deer," said Sugar, holding up a pair of dark bundles. "This is the deer, I think."

"Or the man," said Brooke.

"More meat than man," said Sugar, raising the bundles to shoulder height.

Brooke nodded and held out the knife to the boy. He held it by its blade, leveling the handle with the boy's belly and bouncing it up and down.

"It's a good thing," said Brooke, "to let a man be buried properly as possible. You're doing them a service." He jiggled the knife's blade, trembling the handle. "You'll be doing us a favor too, and we'll all be safer for it."

Finally, the boy accepted the knife.

"Just the teeth?" he said.

"No time for the skeletons," said Brooke. "And besides, we couldn't carry all of this, even if we wanted to."

Sugar dug a small hole with his fingers and slid in the gory bundle. The boy was wiping his hands in the grass, on his shirt, on the bark of the trees around them. He had vomited, but finished the job. Brooke was separating the fresher bundles from the rotten ones. They were all but set to go.

Sugar placed dirt over the bundled teeth, and then grass. The bodies leaning against the trees seemed to watch it all.

"Rest," said Sugar.

"Are there going to be more men?" said the boy.

"There will always be more of someone or something," said Brooke.

Sugar was silent and watching the hole.

"I don't want to do that again," said the boy.

"You probably won't have to," said Brooke. "But you might have to."

"Can we eat?" said the boy.

"Not here," said Brooke.

"Can we go somewhere and eat?" said the boy.

"You've got an appetite after all that?" said Brooke.

The boy nodded, ran his hands across his shirt once more. They had not eaten for some time and the hunger was beyond thinking about.

Sugar unclasped his hands and set his eyes in the direction of the treetops.

"What's he looking at?" said the boy.

"Everything and nothing in particular," said Brooke. He hoisted two of the fresh bundles onto his back and kicked through the blankets once more, looking for the freshest one.

"What are you looking at?" said the boy.

Sugar lowered his eyes to the boy and said he was looking at nothing but whatever it was the trees were doing.

"Is that where the ghosts went?" said the boy.

Sugar shook his head. "They're right there," he said, pointing at the bodies, and then at the small, fresh hole near his feet.

That night, the sun did not set. Sugar placed a strip of fabric over his eyes. Brooke slept on his stomach, his face buried in his elbow. The boy sat awake and watched the trees bend and heard them creak and imagined he heard men approaching from all directions. He heard laughter. Then a twig as it broke. He listened for more, for the hiss of those sounds fading out to confirm them, but heard nothing. It was as if the enormous quiet of the woods around him consumed any possible sounds, growing stronger, more present, more oppressive and huge. He nudged a rock with his toe to provoke a faint scraping, the mild tremble of a rock turning against the earth. As quickly as it rose the sounds were gone. Brooke shifted, rocked his hips. The boy was not afraid of anything in particular, but he was impatient to know what was coming. What was after them and when would it get there? What were they after and would they achieve it?

A black bird curved into view overhead and tilted toward a tall branch. Settling, it picked between its toes and squawked at nothing in particular. It lifted just as suddenly and curved toward the boy and Brooke and Sugar. It landed near their bundles and hopped. The boy watched it hop and tilt and examine the bundle. It pecked a small tear in the corner of the bundle, where the darkest blood had gathered. It pulled something from the bundle and tapped it a moment with its beak before going back in again with another quick peck. The boy toed the rock near his foot again, this time hooking it with his toe and drawing up his leg to bring the small rock to his hand. The bird hopped back and tilted its head. It stepped to the left and turned, as if examining the woods around them. Finally, it turned back toward the bag and pecked again and the boy loosed the rock. It struck the ground and the bird rose only to land again a foot or so away from the very same bundle. The boy drew another rock to his hand with his other foot. The bird seemed to watch him, its head tilted, its eyes blinking and fixed. It pecked at the bag

37

and tapped its beak. It pecked again and the boy slung the rock, harder this time, with an audible exhalation. It struck the now extended wing of the rising bird.

The bird struggled in the dirt for a moment before trying to lift again and collapsing from the pain or the insufficient strength in its wounded wing. The boy rose and was on the creature before it could regather. Brooke rocked and Sugar did not stir.

The boy took the small head of the bird between his thumb and forefinger and held its body in the crook of his opposite arm. He angled the neck of the bird in an attempt to snap it but instead the bones seemed to slip and the pressure between his fingers cracked something in the skull of the creature instead, which sent it twitching and spinning back to the dirt. Brooke stirred then, kicking one boot out and reaching his palm to his face. The boy did not want help but wanted instead to know if he could eat on his own, if he had learned something and what he had in him and what he did not. He felt embarrassed to have dropped the bird and to have it struggling so pathetically there before him. Its wing wounded, its skull partially caved in or cracked like the shell of an egg, it seemed to be trying to gather itself up and again make an attempt at flight. After a few quiet steps he was back on the crippled creature and gripping its body and struggling wings with one hand while pinching the base of its skull between his thumb and forefinger, once again. But the neck was soft; it only bent and slipped when he angled to break it.

"Stop torturing it," said Sugar. He was on his knees and rolling one of the stained blankets he'd gained from yesterday's piles.

"I'm not," said the boy. The bird's visible eye was wide and still, calm-seeming. Matter-of-factly, it watched the boy, the woods, the dirt, as the creature writhed and pumped its body toward escape. The boy applied his palm and full grip to the bird's head, shutting out the light. He wrenched the handful in a small circle away from his own body. The neck did not snap, but grated and ground like dirt in a blanket before the bird set to convulsing and the boy lost its body again. It pumped against the dirt and sent up rings of dust into the sunlight angling at their camp. The boy set himself before it and wiped the sweat from his brow and was nearly set to cry before Sugar approached and cut the neck of the bird in a circle until the head fell back into the dust and stained where it came to rest. He tossed the body into the woods and went back to his blanket and the bundles he would tie it to.

"You had a knife," said the boy. "I didn't have a knife."

"I told you to stop torturing it," said Sugar.

"But I didn't have a knife," said the boy. "You did and that's what made it easy."

"Why were you pitted against a bird?" said Sugar.

The boy had moved toward the woods now, in the direction of the bird's abandoned body.

"It was after our meat," said the boy.

"It couldn't have taken much," said Sugar.

He was watching the boy now, who was circling the base of tree after tree for the bird's body and coming up with nothing.

"You won't find it like that," said Sugar, but the boy did not let up.

"Imagine my throw," said Sugar. "Trace the line extending from me exactly as you imagine it. Don't bother yourself with where it might have gone. Picture exactly where it went and start there."

39

"I can't remember your throw," said the boy, without looking up, moving in circles around the base of each tree, one after the other.

"Don't remember it, just picture it. Just picture it in your head and follow that picture exactly."

Finally, the boy stopped and walked back to stand near Sugar, who was still and watching the boy with his hands at his sides.

"Is this where we were?"

Sugar did not respond.

The boy stood a moment then walked a hard line toward the woods.

"It's here," he said, lifting the headless carcass of a small black bird.

"See?" said Sugar.

"There's really no meat on it," said the boy.

"I know," said Sugar.

The boy let the bird fall.

"You don't want it?" said Sugar.

"I just wanted to get it and have that be easy," said the boy.

"You didn't have to try hard to find it," said Sugar.

"You told me where it was," said the boy.

Sugar shook his head.

Brooke was up then and packed in no time at all. He paused at the bird's head and rolled it with the toe of his boot. Sugar was smoking against a tree with his bundle and blanket at his feet and the boy was squatted nearby, drawing in the dirt with a fingertip.

"Whatever it was that got you, got you good," said Brooke. "You're more horse than boy."

The boy looked at his waist, his smooth hands.

"What do you mean?"

"Nothing bad," said Brooke. "I loved my horse."

"Where's your horse now?" said the boy.

Brooke shrugged. "Died," he said.

"I'm sorry," said the boy.

Sugar stubbed his cigarette.

"I think I'd like to learn more about you," said Brooke.

"I told you," said the boy, "I don't know any more than you." He itched the back of his skull, ran the length of a finger along the lobe of his ear.

"Yes, you did," said Brooke. "But if we were to know someone who might know something, you wouldn't be opposed to us asking around about you, right?"

"Who do you know?" said the boy.

"Just someone who knows things," said Brooke. He pulled an edge of meat from one of the bundles and cut its corner loose with the tip of the curving knife.

The boy nodded and Brooke cut him a piece too.

"We're killing time anyway," said Brooke, "and trying to keep ourselves moving. We might as well head toward him, and see what he might be able to bring to bear on the situation."

Sugar was bent at the waist, a hand on either knee, gulping air and holding his eyelids shut while Brooke went on.

"And maybe he knows something about the way the boy looks or where he might have come from, something to help us along. It seems as good a plan as any."

The convulsions took Sugar again and he loosed another smatter of acid and mucous onto the slick dirt before him.

"I don't care," Sugar managed. "Just leave me."

"We're going," said Brooke, standing at the boy who was still crouched and fingering the dirt. "We're going to our friend and he'll tell us all about you."

"Okay," said the boy. Then, "What's wrong with him?" gesturing at Sugar.

"Stomach," said Brooke. "I don't know. Maybe the meat. Or it's just early and he's unsettled."

The sun was nearly raised and the woods were coming to bloom around them. A handful of birds in the trees just above were mocking the boy or mourning their dead or crying out for something, there was no knowing what. The boy threw a small rock to scatter them, but only one lifted before settling back as it had been.

"Don't," said Sugar. "It's annoying."

He wiped his mouth with his sleeve and kicked some of the dust at his feet onto the mucous and stomach acid he'd abandoned there.

"You insist you have no name?" said Sugar.

The boy shrugged, shook his head.

"Then we'll call you Bird," said Sugar.

"I don't like it," said the boy.

"It suits him," said Brooke, nodding to Sugar.

"But I don't like it," said the boy.

"Bird for now," said Brooke.

"Bird until we find out something different," said Sugar.

"So we're going?" said Brooke.

"We'll go," said Sugar.

They left.

They had little to carry, the bundles of decaying meat and a few stained blankets. They moved quickly and quietly and saw little else throughout the day, other than birds and a few salamanders. Bird could swear the birds were following them, but Sugar assured him it was only his conscience, his self-involvement.

"You're imagining what's happening out there's got anything to do with you," said Sugar. "It doesn't."

"But if someone hurt Brooke you'd chase them down," said Bird. "Because."

"I would," said Sugar.

"So what's to say the birds aren't doing that?"

"Even if they are, it's still got nothing to do with you really. It's out of your hands, and they're no risk to you."

"But I know why they're doing it, and it's me is why they're doing it."

"You put your hand in a lake, withdraw it, and the surface moves for a bit," said Sugar, "it snaps back into place or it ripples on and on. Your involvement ends the moment your hand leaves the water."

"We're here," said Brooke.

It looked no different from any other patch of wood. The boy was not even sure in which direction he should be looking.

"You take Bird," said Brooke.

Sugar placed his hand on the boy.

"After you," said Sugar.

"What do I do?"

"Walk," said Sugar.

"What's Brooke going to do?"

"Wait," said Brooke.

✝   ✝   ✝

As they walked, the woods seemed to bruise. It was nearly, suddenly, evening.

"How far is it?" said Bird.

"Not far," said Sugar.

They were headed toward nothing in particular, it seemed to Bird. Only darkness. Beneath their feet, small stones in the dirt squeaked as they were pressed together. Every now and then one would pop beneath Sugar's heel, but he did not seem to notice.

Bird's toe caught a hidden root and he fell forward, palms out, onto the earth before him. His shin struck the root and his palms stung as they pressed into the small stones hidden beneath a layer of dirt and leaves on the forest floor.

"Can you stay on your feet?" said Sugar.

Bird nodded. He could.

"Then follow."

Sugar took the boy's shoulder and drew him up.

As Bird's hands left the dirt, he unearthed what he'd mistaken for small stones. The yellow edges of two cracked teeth shone up from the earth as a third worked its way from where it had impressed into Bird's palm and fell to join them.

"It's a graveyard," said Bird.

"You'll find that's always the case," said Sugar, "if you pay attention."

Bird was sniffling behind Sugar now, being led by the wrist. Bird said nothing in return, made only a few soft sounds, pausing every now and then to suck air through his nose.

"Are you hurt?" said Sugar.

Bird did not respond.

Suddenly, they could hear water. After a moment they could

see it, too. A silver stream and its heavy movement through the earth.

"We're almost there," said Sugar.

Bird cut his whimpering then and began to tremble slightly against Sugar's grip.

"You should cut all of that before we get there," said Sugar. "If he sees how scared you're acting, he will fuck with you."

The trembling sped up for a bit, then slowed. Sugar could hear the boy breathing in through his nose and out through his mouth. The air was still then.

"We're here," said Sugar.

Before them was a modest camp. There was no smoke. No fire pit. Only a few scattered bundles and a thin man in a suit, sitting upon a rock.

"Sugar," he said, "you've brought a friend."

"His name's Bird," said Sugar.

"For now," said Bird.

"And the baby?" said the man.

"I'm not a baby," said Bird.

"Indeed," said the man. "Sugar, I'm happy for you."

He drew a knee to his chest, set his heel against the rock beneath him.

"Can you tell me anything about Bird?" said Sugar.

"Like what?"

"Where did he come from? Who's his family? Where can we leave him?"

Sugar finally loosed Bird's wrist from his grip, but Bird's hand came back to Sugar's arm only a moment later, clutching his elbow, his forearm, his bicep, his shoulder.

"Don't leave me," said Bird.

"We could get you home," said Sugar.

"I can't tell you anything about him," said the man, "because there's nothing to tell."

"What does that mean?" said Sugar.

"You should keep the baby this time," said the man. "The woods are crying out with all you've left them."

He looked up and around, as if at nothing in particular.

"There is no baby," said Sugar. "Enough about the baby."

"Nothing's gone away. You know that as well as I do."

He was smiling then, eyeing Sugar and Bird, one after the other. He was calm, somehow comforting. It wasn't a feeling Bird recognized. He could not tell if he liked it.

"He'd be better off with his family," said Sugar. "Brooke and I can't help him. He's in danger if he's with us, and we're in danger if he slows us down."

"Most are better off with a family," said the man.

"So help us," said Sugar. "Give me something to go on."

"Keep the baby," said the man. "Make my life easier out here."

"Your life," said Sugar.

"I am being straight with you," said the man. "But you are not being straight with me."

Sugar did not respond.

"Are you?"

"At the very least, you can tell us if the boy has people," said Sugar.

"He does now," said the man. He rose then. He brushed his knees and waved them on.

Sugar protested, but the man moved steadily from the rock and then away from his own camp. He did not look back and he did not register Sugar's increasing alarm.

"He's not ours," said Sugar. "We have nothing for him."

Bird was silent.

"You've put him to death then," said Sugar. "This is on you."

✝   ✝   ✝

When they finally left, Sugar was angry. He was kicking up stones and clumps of dirt without breaking his stride.

"Worthless," said Sugar, over and over again, kicking the earth and scattering teeth.

Bird followed at an uneven clip, hopping and jogging slightly then slowing himself to keep just behind Sugar and out of striking distance.

They were following the same path that had brought them there. Bird spotted the divot where he'd fallen, and he pressed it with his heel.

Sugar paused then, as if he had an idea. He turned to the boy and Bird took a step back, flinched, and Sugar was upon him. He knocked the boy onto his back. The boy swatted his desperate hands and gripped at Sugar's neck until Sugar was able to scoot his knees onto the boy's elbows and, sitting on his chest, pin him at three points to the earth.

"I will gut you," said Sugar, "if you don't tell me this instant where you've come from and what you're after."

Bird coughed and made room for Sugar's grip to tighten.

"You ran away?"

Bird tried to shake his chin. He was wide-eyed, gazing back at Sugar and trying to look plain.

"Someone sent you?" said Sugar.

When he did not respond, Sugar shook Bird. He shook loose the tears Bird was trying to hold back and struck him in the brow with the middle knuckles of his right hand.

"Speak up," said Sugar. "Tell me something to make some sense of all this and I won't break you open and drag you behind us until you've bled out. We'll cut off pieces of you and leave a trail for whoever sent you to find us. And when we deal with them, it will be to mutilate them painfully and leave them to the woods. Then we will deal with your mother and father. We will put your mother's head in a gunny sack and your father's will hang from the side of my saddle."

Bird went back to trying to look plain. Or he was scared enough to be immobilized. Either way, he wasn't crying or fighting, just staring up at Sugar as if there was nothing to do worth doing and nothing at all to hope for in the world.

"What's happened?" said Brooke.

Bird had not heard or seen his approach.

"The boy's got no paths," said Sugar, "no markings of any kind. He's appeared as if from nowhere. He knows nothing." Sugar was pressing his palms against the boy's throat then, holding him to the dirt and squeezing until the boy's eyes bulged and stuttered about in desperation. "We've got nothing to go on other than knowing that we're better safe than sorry. Safer without him. Safer without a mouth to feed and the unknown hanging over us."

"Well," said Brooke, "if you're going to do it, do it." He rubbed his hands together, wiped them along the length of his pants. "But don't drag it out."

Sugar leaned into his hold on the boy's throat and locked eyes with him.

"If you've got something to tell me," whispered Sugar, "you tell me now."

The boy was tense, a short bit of rope tugged from either end, but when Sugar went silent the boy held that way for only a moment longer before releasing into the mud. His eyes wandered from Sugar to Brooke and then to nothing in particular. His air was gone. His throat was bruised and bent. Something was humming up inside of him like the edge of sleep. The sounds of Brooke and Sugar rattled around in his head, little clips of conversation and the sounds of the forest around them now, suddenly, and from before.

When Bird came to, he was not dead. There was a fire at his side, Brooke and Sugar were seated opposite him.

"You," said Brooke, pointing at Bird, "are no help at all."

"You tried to kill me," said Bird. He sat up, coughed, rubbed his throat. He coughed again and loosed a mixture of phlegm, painfully. "You nearly killed me."

"I would have killed you if I was trying to kill you," said Sugar.

"You choked me!" said Bird. He rose, began to search the earth around them for a rock of any size.

"And you produced nothing," said Brooke, "other than sleep. Other than some blood and spit. And now Sugar," he nodded toward Sugar at his left, "he's got nothing much left to try."

"You wanted me dead," said Bird. "I am not safe."

"You're not listening," said Brooke.

"I don't need to listen," said Bird. There were no rocks. Infrequent shocks of dead grass. The dirt was fine where they were, vaguely yellow. The ground was loose and unfamiliar.

"Where are we?" said Bird.

"In between towns," said Brooke.

Finally, Bird's eyes came upon a stick, a few paces off. Not much at all, but substantial enough, maybe, to land a few strikes.

"If you can eat," said Brooke, "you'll feel better."

Bird brought the branch down upon Sugar's defending hand. It fell apart quietly, like ash, and Sugar rose to swat the boy down again.

"Enough," said Sugar. He produced a knife from his waist-band and brought it into the boy's gut.

"No," said Brooke, and the woods filled with thunder then, roaring in the distance at first then rising in volume and velocity like a river run over and borne down upon them.

The earth trembled and the boy collapsed, his hands at the abandoned knife in his gut.

"Horses," said Sugar, and then they appeared.

Dozens of wild horses tore through the camp, tearing their fabrics and trampling their objects flat. Sugar lunged for a tree and began to climb, the muscles of each passing animal thudding against him and bruising his more delicate edges.

Brooke huddled to the ground and was kicked and pressed, broken open about the arms and chest and face. The boy had vanished. The knife too. Sugar climbed the tree up and out of harm's way and swayed with it as the horses passed.

Then it was over. The dust was not settling but the sounds were gone and the trees were rocking back into place. Sugar heard Brooke's cough and knew he was alive. He glanced about for the boy, but did not see him.

"Are you badly hurt?" said Sugar.

Brooke did not answer. He rolled to his side and clutched his gut. He coughed blood and phlegm into the brown mist between them.

"The boy is our concern now," said Sugar, sucking the sharp end of a bone.

"He wasn't a concern and you made him a concern and you've done enough without me," said Brooke. Their meat was raw. They were avoiding fire, resting in the hollows of a large bush.

"I lost my temper," said Sugar.

"You lost your sense, but it doesn't matter," said Brooke. "What was there to know about the boy? What was said?"

"Nothing," said Sugar. "This is what I've been trying to say."

"Can't be nothing," said Brooke. "What were the words?"

"I was told there was nothing to tell," said Sugar.

"Are you my brother?"

Sugar cocked his head, examined Brooke, then nodded.

"In order to work with you I need to know everything you're working with," said Brooke. "In order to be at your side I need to know what you are thinking and reacting to. Otherwise…"

"I'm telling you the truth," said Sugar.

"There was nothing to tell?" said Brooke.

"Nothing. And the boy seemed frightened."

"I imagine it would be a frightening thing to hear. That's all that was said?"

"I asked if he had people."

"And?"

"And I was told he does now."

"Well," said Brooke, "he did anyway."

The horses had left them with nothing. They had borne down upon them like a plague. The boy was gut stuck, bleeding out somewhere in the dark. The two brothers would continue on through the woods and stop at the next town. Whatever they could find. They would acquire horses and cooked food. They would find work and get two beds in exchange. They would build from the ground. They would be spotted. If anyone was looking for them, they would be found and approached within a few days' time, as they figured it.

51

✝ ✝ ✝

The boy was being dragged in the dark and everything was wet. His arms hurt, and his shoulders and elbows. He opened his eyes and the stars above him stretched across the sky like lightning. His arms were above his head and his legs were held up off the ground by something dark, only a few feet in front of him. He could hear the croak of a wooden gear and a man's cough.

"Brooke?" said the boy, and everything stopped. The stars snapped back into place. A hand came down upon his mouth and a stranger's face materialized. Black dirt articulated the cracks at its eyes.

"It's awake," said the face. "Is it hungry and cold?"

The boy was cold but could not detect hunger, though he was uncertain of when he last ate.

"No," said the boy. He tried to sit up but his gut would not allow it. He was overwhelmed with pain then. He clutched his stomach and found blood there and a sensitivity to touch that made him squirm against the earth and fight the instinct to bend back up and double over.

"It's wounded," said the face. "It's bleeding."

"Who are you?" said the boy. "Are you the man from before?"

"I have a voice," said the face. "I have a body and a mind and a face." It smiled at the boy. The eyes were yellow. The teeth were few. The lips were scabbed and bloody.

"Are you going to help me?"

"It depends," said the face. "Is it sick?"

"I don't think so," said the boy. "I'm hurt."

"When was it hurt?" said the face, a few steps back now, circling to the boy's right side.

"I don't know," said the boy. "Not long ago."

"How was it hurt?" said the face.

52

"I don't know," said the boy.

"It was stabbed!" said the face.

"That's right," said the boy.

"In the gut," said the face.

"It feels like that," said the boy.

"So it could be foul and sick to eat," said the face.

"What could?" said the boy.

"Its gut," said the face.

"Please don't eat my gut," said the boy.

"Won't help, *please*. If I cook it long enough, will it still be foul and sick to eat?"

"If you cook me, they'll come for me. They'll see your fire."

"They?" said the face, unflinching, crowding the boy's right ear with its breath.

"The killers I ride with."

"It rides nothing with no one," said the face, "but bleeds in the dirt until I find it and bring it home."

The boy realized then that he could not lift his legs or lower them. They were fastened to whatever dark object was before him. A cart or a wheelbarrow, he couldn't make it out in the dark. He tried again to sit up, but the pain pressed him back down like a stone to the chest.

"It has nothing and no one and nowhere to go," said the face. "It is like a little mouse in the leaves."

"I'm a bird," said the boy.

"A little bird, yes, maybe, and I am a snake or a fish, and I am a lucky one."

The face vanished and the wood croaked once again and the boy was dragging through the leaves as before. A rock passed under him, pulling his shirt up and scratching a painful line from his hip to the center of his back.

53

The trees grew dense until the stars were gone and there was nothing around him except the sounds of the cart and of his being dragged.

They were headed downhill; the boy could feel the pull of gravity, their slight increase in speed, and the ache in his gut as his weight pressed down upon it.

"We're home," said the face, and a stone was slid open to reveal a kind of darkness that has never seen light. It was textured, thick, and pulsing. The boy lifted his arms to swing out at any approaching sounds, but nothing came. He attempted to curl up again but the pain was more than he could bear. He curled his hands into fists and imagined two stones. He pictured a rock breaking into the face, and then the face and its body collapsing there and still forever. He pictured his own body rising up and carrying itself back out into the night.

It was days before they found a town. Uneventful days, filled with bitterness and loaded silence between them. The town was standard. Sugar and Brooke found a bar and found it empty of patrons.

"We're not heavy drinkers," explained the bartender.

"What do you do?" asked Sugar.

"We're religious," said the bartender, "mostly. And we like games. Or most of us do. Every town has a few folks who keep to themselves."

"What's that mean, you like games?"

"It's just something most of us can agree on."

"What kind of games?"

"Can we have two house wines?" said Brooke.

The glasses were set before them and filled. Then the

bartender explained, "Stick and ball games, some. Cards. We're active." He held out his forearm to display his vascular build, as well as the scarring that ran from elbow to wrist. "I'm a slider," he said. "I know it's not good for me, but I get excited. I can't help myself." He drew a stool from behind the bar and set his foot upon it. He cuffed his trousers to mid-calf and displayed the swollen ankle of his right leg. It was purple and white, like a drowned man's.

"That was a misstep that I fell into," he explained. "Hard."

"A committed player," said Brooke. He raised his glass, first to the bartender and then to his brother. Sugar did not raise his glass, but turned back to the bartender and asked the name of the particular game that had cost him his ankle.

"I'll be back in fighting shape soon enough," said the bartender.

Brooke drank, elbowed his brother, but Sugar kept his eyes on the bartender.

"Do you rent rooms?"

The bartender shook his head and pointed across the road.

"That's there," he said.

A building opposite the bar held roughly the same shape, though the porch sagged slightly and the windows were dirty beyond being able to see into.

"How's a place like yours stay open if no one in your town drinks?" said Brooke.

"Travelers, mainly," he said. "And it's not no one, but most."

Brooke finished his drink and Sugar slid his full glass toward the opposite edge of the bar.

"Won't be needing it," said Sugar.

"You're sure?" said the bartender.

Sugar nodded. "Consider us one of yours," he said. "We'll be here a bit and I'd like to try on the life of an insider."

The bartender chuffed, took up the wine glass, and tilted its edge toward Brooke. Brooke waved his hand and rose from the stool beneath him.

"Excuse him," he said, patting Sugar on the shoulder. "Without a proper bed, he gets strange and over-serious. Why don't you hold onto that drink. We'll head across the way and secure a room, then settle up once we've finished our first round."

"Of course," said the bartender.

In the street, Brooke stopped Sugar with a slug to the gut. Bent over, Sugar looked plaintively to his brother and shocked Brooke with the sudden desperation in his eye. He collapsed to his knees, then onto his side in the dirt. Brooke hovered over him.

"What's got into you?" said Brooke. "And where's my brother?"

Sugar watched the townsfolk leave their porches and enter their homes. They could smell a fight, and the two strangers were more than likely armed.

"What aren't you telling me?" said Brooke. He loosed a kick into the middle of Sugar's back, which was curved and exposed from his position. Sugar bent backward and set one hand to protect his spine while the other stayed at his gut, holding it dearly.

"We can keep going on like this," said Brooke, "in front of the clouds and everyone. I can pound you all day and you know it. You've never set against me in two lifetimes and come out on top and that's just the facts of the situation. Either you tell me what's gotten into you or I break you open a bit and see if it doesn't come sliding out."

56

"I'm carrying something," said Sugar.

"Go on." Brooke tapped his heel in the dirt to loose a clump of wet grass, the last bit of the woods still clinging to them.

"I was told I've got something inside me," said Sugar.

Brooke nodded.

"We can get it out," he said.

"I was told not to get it out," said Sugar. "I was told explicitly not to." He was not looking at his brother. He was staring down the lane to where the rowed storefronts and home fronts angled toward one another and vanished into the light. "It felt like a warning."

"We'll get it out," said Brooke. "Everything will be as it always has been. Now get up."

Slowly, Sugar lifted himself, his eyes still locked on the horizon.

Brooke bent to help Sugar and Sugar leaned into the hands that found purchase at the moist pits of each arm.

"You'll be okay," said Brooke. "I've got you."

Bird woke when his wing broke. It had been a steady fall, a straight for the canyons dive, and only some faint part of him knew that it wasn't real, that he would wake and be free of the panic that was riding him, rushing his breath and heartbeat and making him sweat. But then the pain in his wing shot through him and he was in complete darkness again. The daylight and the vast horizons and the deep canyons carved by a steady stream of blue water and all the lush trees, it all vanished and he could see nothing. Only darkness. He could only hear the soft sound of something tearing, and could feel on some basic level that it was the skin of his right forearm. Something sharp was drawing a shallow cut and working the skin loose, and he was tied and broken and without recourse.

He screamed. Nothing about the situation changed. He pleaded into the darkness and the same held true. He swung his left arm and struggled with his right, which seemed pinned or fastened in place and would not budge. His flailing left arm found no company.

What was happening to him continued to happen until he was out of tears and collapsing back into a dream of sawdust and pine needles and wolves gathering at the trunks of each and every tree.

The keeper of the inn was an old maid of the tobacco chewing kind. She spit what she could into a brass pot near the ledger, and the rest hung at her chin between a stray hair and a scar, thick and marbled like lard.

"I'm Brooke," said Brooke, "and this is Sugar."

"Twice the fee for two," she said.

"Same as two rooms?" said Brooke.

"Same," she said.

"That doesn't seem exactly fair," said Brooke.

"Maybe it isn't," she said. She was even in pitch and unmoving, perched on a stool behind the counter and shifting only to bring the brass pot a few inches from her lip and let loose what was filling the basin of her mouth.

"I'll be straight with you," said Brooke, "and tell you that we were hoping we might be able to owe you some work or a favor of some kind, in exchange for a room. We've been in the woods for weeks now."

"Months," said Sugar.

"Months," said Brooke. "We're hard workers and we can commit ourselves to just about any task."

"That your wife?" said the keeper of the inn.

"My brother," said Brooke.

Sugar removed their only weapon—a small blade he'd sheathed in the front leather of his half-inch-thick belt. He placed it on the counter and let his hands fall to his side.

"How about a challenge?" said Brooke, "if a favor won't suit you."

The old woman stared back at him, unflinching, circling her jaw.

"From behind the counter, which of the two of you can get closer to my body without piercing me from across the room." Brooke took several steps to place himself against the far wall.

"You strike me, you lose," he said. "You get closer than my brother without doing so, and we'll come back when we've got some money."

"Two throws a player," said the woman. "I don't have much experience with a knife."

"Two throws then," said Brooke. "Sugar, why don't you join her behind the counter there."

"You have to untwist that wire," said the woman.

A coil of wire was threaded between two copper loops, keeping the waist-high door at the end of the counter cinched shut.

Sugar's fingers were trembling slightly. He wasn't nervous, but still sore and uncertain.

The woman watched his hands work the wire and declared that she would go first.

"It's my roof and my wall," she said.

Brooke nodded, and Sugar unthreaded the wire and joined her.

She did not rise from the stool, but took the knife from the counter and held it a moment. She let it lower her hand, bounced it a bit. She held it by the blade, then the handle. She held its edge before her eye, then its handle. She brought her arm back and sprung it forward as she loosed the knife. It plunged into the wall a foot or so to the left of Brooke's neck and held there.

"You'll announce the throw next time," said Brooke, unshaken.

Sugar retrieved the knife and rejoined the woman.

"I'm throwing," said Sugar.

The knife appeared half a foot from the scar left by the woman's throw, just to the left of Brooke's neck. Brooke smiled. The vein in his neck swelled just slightly with each heartbeat.

Sugar retrieved the knife and rejoined the woman.

She did not rise from the stool. She took the knife from Sugar and held it a moment. She let it lower her hand, bounced it a bit. She held it by the blade, then the handle. She held its edge before her eye, then its handle. She brought her arm back and sprung it forward as she loosed the knife. It plunged into the wall halfway between Sugar's scar and the left edge of Brooke's neck, and held there.

Sugar retrieved the knife and rejoined the woman.

"I'm throwing," said Sugar.

The knife appeared then just at the left of Brooke's neck. When he exhaled, his flesh pressed against the blade.

"A winner," said Brooke.

The woman shook her head.

"Three throws," she said. "I said three."

"You undoubtedly said two," said Brooke, removing the small knife from the wall and joining them at the counter.

Sugar stood beside the woman, sporting a vague grin.

"Three," she said. "My roof and my rooms and my wall."

"How will three not turn into four?" said Brooke.

She shook her head, spit into the pot.

"Can you give me a shave, Sugar?" said Brooke.

Sugar nodded.

"Three a player then," said Brooke.

He took his place back at the wall, aligning himself with Sugar's final scar.

The woman did not rise from the stool. She held the knife in her palm. Let it lower the hand, bounced it a bit. She held it by the blade, then the handle. She held its edge before her eye, then its handle. She brought her arm back and sprung it forward as she loosed the knife. It plunged into Brooke's right thigh, hilt deep.

"You win," she said.

Something was eating. In the darkness, there was nothing but the pain in his arm and gut and the slurping and gnawing ringing out as if against stone. That's what it was. They were in stone. Encased in stone like at the bottom of a canyon. The bottom of a canyon with only a canyon above. His one arm was still mobile and relatively painless. He reached over himself to touch the outer layer of his opposite arm. Bending ached his gut, and touching made the whole arm scream. But he was silent. Tears came, but no sound. Only the sounds of it eating, coming from all around him. As if the boy were thinking it, rather than hearing it. What should have been flesh was rough, wet tissue, like the dense pile of leaves on a forest floor. His left hand recoiled. The eating sounds ceased and the stone moved again. Moonlight lit the cavern walls, Bird's broken body, the cart to which he was tied, and then he was sealed away as before.

Brooke sank to sitting, pulled the blade from his leg, and the windows of the inn exploded with gunfire. Sugar struck the floor and met Brooke's eyes from across the room.

"No," cried the woman, "not the windows and walls."

The gunfire did not cease until she had set to cursing into the palms of her hands and crying just a little and the two brothers had joined one another behind a sagging couch near the center of the room. They had only the blade, slick with Brooke's blood.

Soon they heard boots on the planks of the porch and a voice that called out, "Toss what you've got and rise up slowly."

The boots found their way into the main room, an innumerable cluster of bumps, knocks, and creaks, settling then to silence.

Brooke wiped his blood on the knee of his britches and shook his head to Sugar, who rose up slowly, hands in the air.

Before him stood a line of eight unrecognizable faces, and then that of the bartender. Six-shooters in fourteen hands and shotguns in the remaining four.

Brooke was bleeding through his fabrics. His foot twitched at the ankle.

"My brother's got only a knife," said Sugar. "And I've got nothing."

"Step out from behind the seat," said the leader, a man in a brilliant white button-up topped with a loose brown vest. He bore no signifying marks or pins. He appeared roughly forty years of age, give or take a few years. He was hard-faced and scarred at the chin. "Do it now," he said, evenly.

Sugar did as he was told. He did not glance at Brooke, who was attempting to steady his foot and gain a clear head.

"The other too," said the leader.

A skilled shot nicked the blade of the knife as it landed a foot or so to the left of the couch. It skittered and spun to the far wall and a young boy near the end of the line apologized.

Brooke's hands emerged first. Then the back of his head, his shoulders, and the broad black back of his leathers.

"Turn," said the leader.

"Can't," said Brooke, his hands gripped to the couch's back. "I'm pierced and bleeding."

"Go around and see," the leader said to the man beside him. An older man in a worn black top hat, striped whites, and suspenders set to examine Brooke.

"We've got them," said the boy.

"He's bleeding all right," said the man in the top hat, looking back at his party from the couch's left edge.

"I had them," said the innkeeper, rising from behind the counter. "I had them both and you came to us like this and bore apart my walls."

"Marjorie, we do apologize."

"Apologies won't keep out the wind and the mosquitoes," she said. "This is nothing but a waste on your part and a loss on mine."

"Take them," said the leader, signaling with the barrel of either pistol for his men to approach the brothers.

The man in the top hat lifted Brooke to standing and pulled his wrists together before him. He lashed them with a worn bit of coil while the others set upon Sugar.

"I'd like to request a cell near my brother's," said Brooke.

"I'm sure you would," said the leader, tucking his guns behind his belt and releasing the tension in his shoulders.

"For comfort in a new place, and for the discussion of our defense," said Brooke.

Sugar was blank, led to the door by a ring of four men. The face of each blended with the next. Sugar buckled slightly as he disappeared through the door.

"Plus, he's sick and should be minded," said Brooke.

"The thing is," said the leader, stepping to Brooke finally with a grin like a lightning bolt. "There's no cell. No defense. And no one at all to pay either of you any mind."

He startled then, as if to slug Brooke, but paused as the bound man flinched. When Brooke recovered, the leader plunged a thumb into the fresh wound at Brooke's thigh, sending Brooke to the floor again. Then the leader turned to take his leave.

The remaining four men lifted Brooke and led him through the door where two stagecoaches, each drawn by a set of four horses, were waiting. The lanterns on the stagecoaches were lit. The sun was finally preparing to set. The horses were newly shod and freshly brushed, as if prepared for a journey of some length.

Brooke was brought to an empty stagecoach, and his mind settled to thinking of Sugar in the other, and whether or not his brother would meet the opportunity to take the gun from one of his men the moment it presented itself.

The men set him on a low bench at the back of the wagon. They sat around him, two across from him and one at either side.

If he had not recently been stabbed, he wouldn't have startled. If Sugar had not acted out upon Bird, they would not have come to this town. The men and the innkeeper, he realized, had been working separately toward the same end. Their plan was known, or at least its most relevant parts. A pistol butt broke into the flesh above his ear and sent him into the lap of the man at his left. From that position, he could make out only the sky and a pair of large red rocks on the horizon. He felt blood at his neck. The sun was behind them, disappearing into the earth. As the stagecoach began to move, he could then see the town, shrinking behind them. Its walls and facades, as they were broken apart, pulled outward by faintly visible ropes, and folded at the middle, back toward the earth. The town was splitting apart like a radish root in a dish of water. In the shadows at its edge, he imagined he saw the phantoms of men, working.

The rock did not move. Time passed and more time passed and still the rock did not move. Then, finally, the rock moved.

When Brooke awoke, his head was still in the lap of the man beside him. That man was watching something out the window with a plain look on his face. He startled when Brooke shifted, then forced his lips back to flat and nodded at the prisoner. Brooke nodded back.

"You are not comfortable with prisoners," said Brooke.

The man did not speak.

No one spoke.

The driver glanced behind him to check the faces of the other men. Through the window, all that could be seen was the dark purple of the dirt and yellow plants straining from between the rocks. The shadows on the horizon, he imagined, were the great red rocks that decorated the immense desert between this town and the next. The stars were out.

Brooke checked both windows, but saw no sign of the second wagon. He listened, but heard nothing. It was at least half a day if they were headed to the nearest town. Anywhere else would be much longer.

"Is there food?" said Brooke. "Are we to eat?"

The men did not respond. They rode in silence and time bore on.

"I find silence in the desert as pleasurable as the next man," said Brooke, "but this is intolerable. I'd like at least to know why I'm here and what I'm answering to and where I'm going."

"You're answering for those you've killed, Brooke," said one of the men sitting across from him. This man was the top-hatted man from before. His look was less pleasant now, as he had begun to sweat, and his eyes were sunken from either weariness brought on by travel or a road-sickness he was making no bluster about.

"Which of those?" said Brooke.

"It hardly matters to us," said the man. "Murder is murder." He coughed into a kerchief. "By our punishment, you answer for one and you've answered for them all."

"You plan to put us down then?"

"You'll be put down in due time."

"And my brother?"

The man to the left of the top-hatted man began to sneer at Brooke and did not break eyes with him.

"I don't much like the way your man is looking at me," said Brooke.

"And we don't much like you, Brooke. We'll take a particular pleasure in delivering you, and we'll take a particular pleasure in seeing you put down. Your *brother* as you call it, is carrying a child. As decency demands, we'll bring it to term, deliver the child, then deal with the creature."

Brooke did not speak.

Bird woke, and was covered in fur. The room was lit brightly and warmly and there was music playing, a soft piano and a lagging violin. He couldn't place the sounds then, but would come to know them dearly.

"You're awake, sweet boy," said a voice. A bearded man in glasses and a vest and a bowler appeared over Bird. "You'll notice we took your arm."

Bird's arm had been lopped off, just above where would have been an elbow. He was bandaged and the bandage was leaking only slightly from over-saturation.

"It wasn't our preference to do so, but it was more infection than appendage when we found you."

"What infection?" said Bird. "I was gut-stabbed."

He realized then that he could bend, as he was sitting up and addressing the man.

"I'm John," said the man, sitting at the edge of the bed into which Bird had been bundled. "You're lucky we found you when we did."

"What happened to my arm?"

"Buried," said John, "in the yard."

"But why?" said Bird.

"I told you. The infection—"

"What infection?"

"Your arm was incredibly infected, boy. It tends to happen when the skin's removed."

"The skin?"

"It's too horrible to relive, perhaps," said John. "I was a war man. I spent time fighting alongside men who died both proudly and cravenly, men who cried and men who prayed. I know about torment. About men at their end. But what you went through is singular. No man should know it, let alone a mere child."

"It was eating me," said Bird. "Wasn't it?"

"Some of you," said John, removing his bowler. "It seemed primarily interested in the skin."

"I'd like to kill it," said Bird.

"I'm sure you would," said John. "But I'm sorry to say it's been killed and boxed and sold. You'll eat with us, stay with us as long as you like, and grow fat on the food its corpse paid for. That will have to be your justice."

"I don't want anything other than for it to be dead," said Bird.

"Long dead," said John.

"What was it?"

"Just a creature," said John. "Just a man gone to beast. It hardly matters at this point."

"What sounds are those?" said Bird.

"My wife and daughter," said John. "We thought we might try to play you awake. Are you hungry?"

"I don't know."

"Well, try to eat then and see what happens. Can you rise?"

Bird shifted his body to dangle his legs from the edge of the bed. He leaned forward, set his feet to the ground and pushed from his wrist to set his weight upon his legs. There was still a pain in his gut, but nothing like before.

"Was I infected in the gut?"

"No. But stabbed through."

"I knew that part."

"I suppose you did."

"Am I safe?"

"As safe as any of us are."

"Is that safe?"

"You're safe, yes. There were three of us, and now four."

Bird was able to take one step, and then several before buckling and falling to one knee.

"Or three and a half," said John.

Just outside of the room Bird found himself in, there was a table set with silver and porcelain and several candles. Corroded copper hung from metal hooks. Stirred butter sat in a bowl. A woman sat at the piano in the living room, just beyond the half-wall hedging in the table. Next to her stood a short girl in a white bit of clothing.

The girl lowered her violin and turned to greet Bird with bright excitement. Her mother played a few resolving notes on the piano, then closed the cover over the keys and scolded her daughter.

"Mary, it's important each time to play the measure through."

"He's awake," said Mary, pointing to Bird, who was using the dinner table to keep himself from swaying, leaning his right hip into it in a way he figured to be subtle.

"Did you sleep well?" asked Mary's mother. She was stiff, turned at the waist with her knees still pointing forward, her foot still on the piano's pedal, sustaining the note.

"I had nightmares," offered Bird. The urge to lean and the weakness in his legs was finally too much, and he sank into the chair at the head of the table.

"O you kind gods, cure this great breach in his abused nature! The untuned and jarring senses," said John.

"He's hungry," said Mary, placing her violin in its case on the floor and coming to join Bird at the table. "Can we eat?"

"Play something, Martha, to ease us into meal time," said John, and his wife happily obliged.

Bird knew nothing before like the sound of that piano resonating within the wooden walls of this new home.

"What did you dream about?" said Mary.

John wrapped a towel around the handle of the iron pot boiling on the stove. He lifted it and settled it onto a piece of carved wood between his daughter and the young boy.

"We could start with his name," said her father, "maybe where he comes from, before we settle into exploring the hells of a tortured mind."

"What's your name?" said Mary.

"Bird," he said.

John stirred the pot and set a biscuit on Bird's plate.

"You have to wait until it cools," said John. "You're eyeing it like a hound."

"Sorry," said Bird. He tried to reach for the biscuit with an arm that wasn't there, then blushed and tears came and he went at the biscuit with his other.

"There's no shame in hunger," said John.

"Where do you come from?" said Mary, pulling her legs up into her chair to pad her seat.

She wasn't a pretty girl. Her eyes bulged like a victim's. Her hair was in a tight braid, narrowing down the back of her dress. She had a high forehead and an unclean complexion. But she was genuine in her interest and kind in her phrasing.

"A farm just beyond the mountains," said Bird. He pushed the biscuit against his plate to break it into fourths, but it was buttery and slick. It slid from his hand and would not steady.

"Which one is that?" said John. "You're not Tully's boy?"

"No," said Bird, "but I... I think we knew a Tully."

"Tully's fine to do business with," said John, "but not much for company. That's good playing, Martha."

Martha nodded with her chin and body toward the piano, leaning into something slow and practical. It blended neutrally with the atmosphere of the room and caused neither a foot to tap nor an ear to lose its conversational footing.

"I didn't know him well," said Bird.

"Well, you're young," said John. He came up behind Bird and reached to his plate with a spoon in order to break the biscuit in half. He then sat in the seat beside his daughter and lifted her braid with one hand. "You think we're any closer to cutting this?"

She shook it free from her father's casual grip.

"Thank you," said Bird.

"Did you see any fighting?" she asked.

"Some," said Bird.

"Did you see any men die?"

"If he did," said John, "is it something he would want to talk about immediately after waking up as he did? Let him breathe a little. Let him eat. His stories will come out with time."

"I... I don't have any stories," said Bird. "I grew up on a very normal farm and my parents were very casual people who did not bother much with towns or neighbors."

"Well there's no company like kin," said John, "although I'm sure your folks did a lot more than you knew at the time. It's the way of parents and children. You'll understand it when you're older."

Bird nodded.

"It's about as unpleasant a segue as I could have mustered,

but I do wonder some about how you wound up in the cave and what might have happened to your parents. Can we take you to them? Can you guide us from the main road?"

"They're dead," said Bird, finally accepting a bit of the warm biscuit into his mouth.

"Oh, no," said Mary.

"Oh," said John, "how? Martha, can you stop for a second?"

Martha nodded without turning, shut up the piano, and rose to join them at the table.

"Bird's got some heavy news and I couldn't make light of it with your lovely playing," said John. "You were excellent, my dear."

"What's the heavy news?" said Martha. She loaded her plate with slop from the pot, then she loaded Mary's. John served himself, then offered a full ladle out to Bird.

"You were saying, Bud?"

"Bird," said Bird.

"You were saying, Bird?"

"They died, my parents. They were killed. Two men killed them. For money. They were killers, the men. They stabbed me and left me for dead and I wandered until I wound up here."

Martha shook her head. She closed her eyes.

"The evils in this world abound," she said.

She tilted her chin toward her lap. When she opened her eyes, there was a softness to them that hadn't been there before. She reached across the table and took Bird's hand. He flinched at first, then accepted the gesture. "Child, you'll live with us until they find and punish the men who did this."

John nodded.

"Do you know anything about them? Their names? Why they

hurt your family? What they looked like? Where they were from or where they were headed?"

"No."

"It's okay," said Mary.

"One of them had a handkerchief, I guess. He was slightly round about the waist. Soft features. A hanging chin. He was the younger of the two."

"The other?" said John.

"He was much bigger. Muscular. He had… a rough look to him."

"Oh," said Mary.

"He had stubble, like you," Bird pointed to John.

"It's been a long weekend," said John.

"And they carried knives in their boots."

"You said they did it for money?" said John.

Bird nodded.

"How did you know?"

"They… brought parts back. They were planning to make some sort of trade, I guess. I heard them. They… they put my mom's head in a gunny sack and my dad's hung from the side of the saddle."

"Whoa," said Mary.

"Now Bird," said Martha, "I know you've been through some kind of hell, but you've got to do your best to keep this thing civil. I won't have Mary waking up with nightmares for weeks to come."

"Sorry," said Bird.

"Sorry?" said Martha. "Sorry what?"

"Don't mess with him, Martha. He's telling a story."

"Sorry for… saying what I said," said Bird.

"She wants you to say ma'am," said Mary.

"I'd like a bit of respect at the dinner table, is all," said Martha.

"Don't mess with the boy," said John.

"I'm sorry, ma'am," said Bird.

"Thank you, Bud," said Martha.

"Bird," said Bird.

"Thank you, young one."

The top-hatted man was named Jim. The other riders had made it clear enough, in spite of their efforts to hide it. Brooke was keeping quiet now, learning what he could from their scattered conversation, and mulling over the news they'd delivered what felt like half a day before. They were deep in the country, deep in the desert. It was cold. Brooke could see his breath. The stars were out and the moon was bright enough to reflect the edges of the enormous rocks articulating the wide expanse in either direction. They were following a thin stream, headed for the arc where two large rocks met. If he was lucky, they would camp and maybe he would see Sugar. If he was unlucky, they were going to bury him in the hollows.

"Jim," said Brooke.

The man turned to him, but did not answer.

"How did you know about Sugar?"

"It's plain as day, rat."

"I'd like you to be kinder," said Brooke. "I've never conde-scended to you. I'm only asking for basic human treatment. I'm not asking for pardon."

"It doesn't matter what you're asking for," said Jim, "or what you're not asking for. It's us who's running things, bloodhound. We'll handle you how we see fit."

The carriage lurched to a halt then and the driver leapt from his perch.

"Get your guns," he whispered.

"What's happened?" cried one of the men.

"Shut it or I'll shut it for you," said the driver.

"Put him in the bench," said Jim, signaling to the men on either side of Brooke.

They lifted him, opened the seat beneath them, and before he could protest with more than a jerk of his bound wrists, he was bent over the mouth of the opened bench and stuffed into a curled-up position. Then he was sealed off. It was all darkness. He pushed against the wood above him. It bowed outward but did not open or burst.

He heard voices then. He heard hooves and the crack of a rifle. He heard yelling, more gunfire. Every sound was amplified by the rocks rising up around them. It echoed out like the first battle of creation. Like life was forming right there in the opening of that hollow.

Then there were bodies on the wagon. It rocked and Brooke slid an inch one way and then an inch back the other. There was the clinking of metal clasps, sacks dragged and dropped. It was a robbery, or they were abandoning him. Everything was flying off the wagon and the men were crawling around on it like spiders, looking for anything and everything to take with them.

"No passenger," said a voice.

"As he thought then," said another.

After only a few moments, the wagon went still and he heard the thuds of boots on sand and then the hoof-falls of horses fading into the distance. He pushed against the wood above him. It bowed again, loosed a little light this time, revealing the unfinished edges of the box around him. A bit of sand slipped in and stung his eyes. He turned his body, pushed with his knees, and was able to get the lid up about an inch or so. He kept at it. With knees and bound hands, then his forehead, he pushed against the lid and bowed it outward until it began to crack. The latch holding it shut would not budge. It was new, though the rest of the bench was splintered and worn. The lock was purchased, maybe, for this particular event. A small honor. The age of the wood was apparent enough. It croaked and creaked as he bowed it. It bent and shuddered and finally broke in a jagged line at the edge of the shining new latch.

He was up then and surveying the damage. The wagon was empty. He could see nothing through the window. He looked around for something sharp, a blade or a bit of broken metal, to remove his bindings. There was nothing. He opened the door of the wagon with his toe, slowly at first. When nothing happened and no sounds came, he pushed it open with his body and he stepped out and onto the foot ladder, lowering himself then down to the sand. The horses had been cut loose, and were gone. The still bodies of his captors decorated the landscape. They were shot, each and every one of them.

Brooke checked them, one by one, for a pulse. Nothing. Nothing. Nothing. Then Jim. Brooke set two fingers to the body's neck and Jim startled, met the other man's eyes with his own. He was pained but had strength left.

"We'll just keep coming," said Jim.

"I know," said Brooke.

"If you can get out of the desert, we'll find you."

"I know," said Brooke.

"We'll hunt you down until—"

Brooke set his boot to the man's throat then, shutting him up. He ground down for only a few seconds before Jim stopped struggling against him. When Brooke reached to check the pulse again, he was met with no resistance.

"How old are you then?"

Sugar did not answer.

"You're an abomination. You know that. A creature."

Sugar did not speak.

"You know that, right?"

The woods were thick around them and thickening. It was dark out and getting darker. They were approaching midnight. Approaching smells that Sugar knew. A kind of air that was familiar.

"You and your brother, you are no more than beasts."

The man opposite Sugar had been talking the entire ride. Nothing could shut him up, not even a direct request from one in his party, though each had tried. The man was needling Sugar, trying to get a response, trying to get a rise. He wanted something from him, but Sugar would not give it. He was thinking only of Brooke. And occasionally of Bird. He figured Bird was dead; if not by the knife then by the power of those horses. But he could not be certain. Brooke would be dead. If those men didn't kill him, Sugar would fight him and one of them would lose. It didn't matter who lost. Every day now with Brooke was all lies and more trouble. And now this. Now he was sick with something rotten in his gut and the whole world making a point of telling him how different and horrible he was.

"And what you got in you is going to be worse than a creature," said the needling man. "It's going to be one of those lumps licking salt off the walls of the barn. You'd be better off drowning it in a bucket than carrying it to term."

Sugar did not answer. He watched the man. He wore a blank expression.

"It'd make better horse food than person. You'll probably die squeezing it out of you. It will probably claw at your insides like a mountain lion."

The wheel of the wagon rode violently over a large stone. The sounds of insects swelled the distance around them.

"Normally, in such a situation, we'd like to have a go at our catch. Out here in the woods alone. It would even be sort of romantic," said the needler. "But you aren't worth unbuckling for. I wouldn't climb inside you with ten extra miles of dick skin."

Two of the corpses had knives in their boots, and the other two had sheaths where knives should have been. The guns were gone. The only shells in the sand were spent. There was no food. No sacks or cases left on the wagon, except for an empty one. It was rawhide and would do to hold water. Brooke took that, as well as the broken bits of leather strap that had once held their horses. He took the bench's wood too, and what he could pry from the walls of the wagon. It was steel and oak, the wagon, so he could only pry enough for maybe two fires, if he was careful with them. He worked as quickly as he could, confident the other men would not return but not wanting to test that theory. When he had gathered what he could gather, he went to the stream and set himself on his stomach before it. He drank for several minutes, cupping the water into his mouth, then lowering his cheek to the sand to breathe a few calming breaths. Finally, he gathered water in the sack, tied it off, and made for the gap between the rocks—right where the wagon had been headed and the best chance he had for catching a path toward wherever it was they were taking him and, it was possible, his brother.

Mary was a good companion. She told stories about bobcats and wild horses. Her father took in animals and nursed the sick ones. They'd owned over a dozen dogs in her lifetime, and she was just now twelve. They currently owned three. One was all black and had lost a paw.

"Just like you," she said.

They were leaning against the horse fence and watching the ponies. They had two mild ponies her father had discovered at a stream near a canyon.

"He saved them," she told Bird.

"I'd like to get it back some day," said Bird, examining his bandages. They were white and clean, rather than soaked in brown and yellow as they had been the day before.

"You won't get it back some day," said Mary, "if I know anything about anything. It's okay, though. Nobody around here minds and there's still plenty you can do."

"It does not always feel gone," said Bird, eyeing approximately where his hand would have been.

"Oh," said Mary, "that's something I read about. That's a special trick your mind is playing. That's interesting. Will you describe it to me? What's it like? How real does it feel?"

"Very real," said Bird, "all the way."

"Isn't that something?" said Mary. "You are like a soldier returned from war. I am like your patient wife who has been waiting all along for you to return. But I am not really like your wife at all, I suppose. You are one of the things John brings home, not exactly a husband."

"I could be a husband," said Bird. "I could be anything."

"Not really," said Mary. "Plus, you are young and a cripple now."

"I'm not," said Bird.

"I don't mean anything by it," she said. "I love the dogs and ponies alike. Dad brings home good things and makes everyone's life better."

"What's that one's name?"

"I call him Little One."

"Because he's the littler."

"Yes."

"And the other?"

"Friendly," said Mary, "but he is not exactly friendly outside of the name. It is more a joke my dad and I make."

The ponies kept their distance of the fence and Bird quickly lost interest. The project of the day was to learn Mary's chores, to follow her around and see what she was responsible for and how he could help, eventually.

"You're healing now," John had said, "and we're happy to care for you until you've got back your strength. After that, everyone who can help out around here, helps out around here. It's only fair."

Bird was learning, though, that Mary didn't take her responsibilities as seriously as one might, given the family's low numbers and all that needed to be done. Her jobs were fairly simple too. Feeding the horses was a matter of sacks and proper distribution. She dragged the sacks instead of carrying them, spilling their contents indiscriminately. She gave the animals ears of corn in unequal amounts. Some got none. She was to feed the dogs too, but she told Bird they mostly fended for themselves. She assured him she would put the scraps from each meal in their bowls, in case they came sniffing around, but there was no need to worry too much about it. They were ungrateful anyway, the dogs. Sometimes they knocked her over if she lingered at their dishes too long. So she made a habit of steering clear of the dogs when she could and pouring kitchen scraps over the back porch, aiming more or less for the dishes below.

Instead of chores, Mary liked to talk and walk and show you things. At least she liked to talk and walk and show him things. He did not know what she would be doing if he were not around to soak her up.

"Dad is a minister but does not preach. Mom is a musician and sometimes she goes to town to play in the church or on a porch near the post office. She used to not talk at all, when she was younger. Dad took her in. She got normal and started to talk more. I used to ask her why she did not talk and she said it was because she did not have a thing to say. It does not make sense to me and seems like a lie. How can we live in this world and have nothing to say about it?"

They were in a field. Grasshoppers the size of biscuits bent long blades of grass back down toward the earth, and sprang up to strike Bird and Mary on the neck, chest, and arms.

Bird was swatting at them, trying to crush the landed ones beneath his boot.

"They do not bite," said Mary. "It's just a hello."

Bird grabbed one from his shoulder and crushed it in his hand.

"Gross," said Mary. "You should be more agreeable."

Bird apologized. He'd never seen anything like it. It looked like a creature. He did not like creatures or things he did not know that came at him.

"Lots of things are going to come at you," said Mary. "It is only the world saying hello."

"I don't agree with you," said Bird.

"Well, I'm right about it," she said.

"Lots of things are not saying hello. They'd like to hurt you. Every man must protect himself."

"I agree with you there," said Mary. She plucked a grasshopper from a blade and held it out to Bird in her palm. "But not here." The grasshopper leapt, but not before eliminating in Mary's cupped palm. "Oh!" She rubbed either side of her hand into the billows of her dress. "He's wet my hand."

That made Bird laugh, seeing her so mildly put out.

"You have a nice look when you're put out," said Bird.

"That's not a nice thing to say," said Mary. She was hurt and it showed in the way she held her face.

"I meant nothing by it."

"Say I look nice all the time."

"You do."

"Say the words."

"You look nice all the time."

"Thank you, little bird."

"You can call me just Bird."

"I know," said Mary. "But you are little. You are one-third bird."

"I won't always be little."

"But you are little now. Even littler than me and I am the littlest."

"What do these things do?" said Bird, nudging the crushed grasshopper with his toe.

"Eat," said Mary, "and hop. They don't have much to go on."

"Then why are there so many?"

"Because there is room for them, I guess," said Mary.

When they were finished in the field they went around to the barn and Bird watched her feed the horses. She made a mess of it. She put no care into it at all. She obviously did care about the horses, though. She said nice, encouraging things to them and warmed their noses with her hands. But she did not do an even job of feeding them and she did not put forth the effort to get each and every one of the seven an ear of corn of their own. She gave extra corn to the littlest one, and the all white one, and one she thought seemed in a particularly good mood. She fed the tan one and the black one with white stockings evenly. Then she got distracted by their water bucket, how full of slop it was, and she playfully scolded the stockinged horse for poisoning the others.

"He's a rascal, you see," she explained to Bird. "He's always up to something sneaky, but it's because he has an active mind and we keep him locked up in here all day."

"I have seen horses before," said Bird.

"Bully," said Mary.

"I saw a mass of horses ride through a clearing like hornets from a nest."

"You saw a stampede," said Mary.

"I saw a stampede," said Bird. "They tried to kill me."

"There you go again," she said.

She dumped the sludgy water in front of the barn and took the bucket to the spigot around back.

Bird examined the horses but did not know what he was looking for. Some kind of kinship. Something that bound them together and made them all horses in the same situation. He spotted nothing but similarities in the ways they moved and held their faces, but even those were fairly distinct from horse to horse when he really thought about it.

Moths broke the sunlight coming through the cracks overhead. Or bats. He could not tell because his eyes were focusing and unfocusing as he moved through the large beams of light striping the barn's interior. He listened for any squeaks or squeals but heard only the sounds of the horses stepping in the grass and breathing and those of Mary making her way back around the barn with the water.

"I like it here," said Bird.

"It is a nice place," said Mary.

It was a bright night, and everything was more blue and white than black, but still Brooke could not make out the trail they might have been taking, or any prints to indicate a proper route. If he'd learned the stars, he could have at least followed them in some vaguely correct direction. But he had not learned the stars. He had not even tried. He might have tried more, he thought. He might have retained a few things here and there, instead of always just doing what he was good at and never learning anything. He cursed himself for being good at things that got you by. He turned back from his wide wandering and decided to follow the water instead. He might have been lost, but at least he would live.

In every direction, it was rock and desert. Small plants cropped up like lint on the horizon, but there was nothing substantial, other than stone and vastness, nothing that would lead him to believe food would be coming his way any time soon. He wasn't particularly hungry, but he would be. For Brooke, it came on strong, and like a seizure, it gripped him and would not let go.

It was funny to him, to die in this way. Alone and for no good reason. Nearly every man he'd killed, he'd killed for a reason, however simple the reason was. And now he would die from bad luck and the world's indifference. It was funny to him, on some level.

He began to list in his head the men and women he had killed in his life. One of them or some of them had come back on him and that had brought him here. It had likely not happened as intended, but the end result would be the same.

There was Jenny's man. The runner. Whatever it was he'd done, Jenny wanted him gone, and she was a high payer and even a sort of friend. And now Jenny was gone and her bar was gone and there was nothing left of the sizable deal they'd made. Taking the man down had not been a particular challenge. They'd found him sleeping beside the very fire he had used to cook his last meal. They positioned his face in the coals and held it there until he ceased to struggle. They had not robbed him because they did not rob when they did not have to. People are sentimental and objects have personal value beyond the knowledge of thieves. They were to be paid and would have had everything they needed, so they left the man's objects to those who would find him. They took his food but that would have been of no use to anyone but themselves after a day or so. It was an easy job, but one that had gone uncelebrated and, as far as Brooke knew, unrumored or spread. It was likely not an associate of Jenny's man that was after them.

Before that there was a constable of some sort. Brooke could not remember the full details of the man's position. He had been on the payroll of a criminal who was doing fine more or less running a small town by a large lake, until he hassled the wrong farmer and got a couple of killers after him. At one point, Brooke and Sugar had been in high demand wherever they'd gone. People needed support, protection. They'd like a gun in their hand, but even more they'd like a gun in someone else's hand, a hand they could control. Brooke understood it. He appreciated it. Decent people had others to look after and could not go hunting folks down for revenge or justice themselves. He and Sugar were not technically decent people. They had one another, but it was because they were brothers and they cared for one another, not out of any kind of necessity or civility.

It was true, the constable of some sort had put up a fight. He even tried to hole up in his home with a set of antique rifles. Brooke and Sugar had finally had to smoke him out, filling his windows with explosive cocktails and setting themselves up to fire on anyone who came tumbling out. They expected him to come from the front door or a window, but the man had held his position. There was very little recognizable left of him in the ashes.

Brooke did not like killing men of high standing because it made people restless. It made them worry that they were not safe, and Brooke and Sugar were far better off with everyone feeling like they were safe. Safe as possible. They'd left that town and never come back. It was entirely possible that the constable's men were those who were after him and his brother. They'd had an official air to them, Brooke's captors. They were self-righteous and clean.

There was little use in this kind of speculation, but he needed something to keep his mind and feet moving as he progressed toward wherever it was that he was going.

Another possibility was the little man who'd razed Jenny's. They hadn't killed anyone that Brooke could remember, but they'd beaten his men and there was reason to be sore about the exchange. The hope had been to leave town and be done with all of it. There was plenty of territory to roam and no reason to ever go back to any particular spot if there wasn't something favorable awaiting them. They weren't about to get in any established person's way over something that was much larger than either him or Sugar.

The stream broke against a large red rock and split in two. Brooke had heard that a lot of the stars in the sky were more or less the same every night, and you could use them as a tool. It did not look that way to him. It looked like a pan full of sand that shook and shook each night after it set.

His mind was wandering. He could not focus. It meant he was tired, but he could not bring himself to stop moving yet. He needed some final something to secure himself in his plan, or to draft a new one. He did not like to wait or give in before a challenge. It was cold out there. He was shivering and wet and getting colder. He did not like the desert.

After several hundred more feet, he fell. He loosed a reasonable amount of wood from his supply and began to pile it into a cone. He could not go on in the cold, tired as he was. There was no shame in collapsing. There was only shame in letting fear or uncertainty give you pause. There was a flint in each of his heels and he removed his boots to get the fire going then slid them back on for additional warmth. They were not safe shoes, but that was part of the pleasure of them. And more than once they'd brought him comfort and a sense of home when there would otherwise have been none. He did not like to wear them down, but emergencies did happen. He warmed his hands and cheeks when the flames finally kicked up. He listened to the fire snapping and the water singing against the rocks behind him. He did not much mind being alone. He wondered if he would be alone forever, or if he would meet Sugar again and then he wondered if they would get over whatever it was that had come between them, and settle into one another once again.

In the mornings, Martha played her piano. Whether or not it was to wake them or to greet them as they woke, it was unclear. Bird's strength was coming back. He thought less and less about the arm, and more and more about eating, sweating, and helping. He kept active. He was normally up before Martha began. He would hear her heels break the silence, then the shift of the key cover and her settling in. He did not know the songs she played, but he often heard John humming them throughout the day. Bird did not want to draw attention to himself by being the first one up, so he listened for John or Mary before making his presence known. It wasn't a worry of his exactly, but something physical. He simply could not lift the blankets until the house was at least half awake.

Sometimes, in the morning, the clouds would look like a plowed field spread across the sky. The sun would come through them and change them and Bird would watch through the small window by his bed. That time of year, there was frost in its corners each morning, like white fur.

Martha would play them right up to breakfast, songs that paused but seemed to have no end. John cooked and served and the songs went on until the plates were loaded. Then Martha joined them. She was tight-lipped and cinched. She sat up like a board.

"We'll cut your hair today, Mary," said Martha, digging into her bacon with a dull knife.

"I like it long," said Mary.

"If we do not cut it, someone will mistake you for a heathen and take you away during the night."

"Martha," said John.

"Martha, none of it," said Martha. "I'm only saying I'd like to clean my daughter up a bit and keep her nice."

"I am nice," said Mary. She was tearing up and not eating her eggs.

"Until you're taken away and all the decency is riven from you," said Martha.

Martha's own hair was spiraled up and held in a bulb at the back of her head. There was no way of knowing precisely how long it was, but Bird was sure it was fairly long, given the thickness of the bulb. She had dark hair you could get lost in. Closer to her head, Mary's hair was like two blonde hands interlocked at the fingers.

After breakfast, John led Mary out behind the house. He carried a small hatchet. Bird followed a few steps behind. Mary was crying and wiping her tears with the backs of her hands. She did not normally cry and Bird was curious at it. It made her appear much younger and smaller than she truly was.

"It will grow back," said John, stopping before a stump.

Mary got on her knees and tilted her face away from the stump. She did not speak. John set her braids on the stump and chopped them more than halfway off with the hatchet. It happened in a single chop. Then the whole thing was over.

John gave the hair to Mary and said she could do what she wanted with it. She wanted to bury it. She did not ask Bird to follow her and did not explain what it was she was about to do. But he followed her and saw it all anyway.

She wandered into the dried-up orchard a few hundred feet from their home. She dug a small pit with her fingers and set the braids in there. She pulled leaves from one of the least dead trees and scattered the leaves over the braids coiled together in the hole like a handful of baby snakes. Then she put the dirt back on top and cried a little more and turned to walk home. Bird thought the funeral was nice and felt his appreciation of it as a kind of warmth throughout his entire body.

"Did you know my name is Isabella?" said Mary.

She and Bird were sitting on the lip of the stonewall encircling the family well.

"I thought it was Mary," he said.

"It's Isabella," said Mary. "John named me Mary when he found me."

"Where did he find you?"

"I can't remember."

"How do you know your name was Isabella?"

"*Is* Isabella," she said.

"How do you know your name is Isabella?"

"I remember that part," she said. "It's the part I remember."

"What else do you remember?"

It was mid-morning. The clouds were low and thick. They seemed to be gathering. Bird did not want a storm. He did not like a storm and would grow more and more afraid until it was over. He had not yet shown this family what he looked like fully afraid and he was starting to think that maybe he would like to go a little longer without showing them.

"Not much. I had a mother who was nice, and I liked her, I think. She called me Isabella. We had a blue and white blanket that sometimes held me and sometimes held corn. I remember touching the corn. What do you remember?"

"From when?"

"From before John found you."

"Nothing, really," said Bird. "I remember I was dragged behind a wagon or a cart for what felt like forever."

"John bandaged you and brought you through the night back to our home," she said. "We were all asleep when you got here and I ran out to greet him and there you were. You were frightful to look at."

"Yeah."

"You were screaming and moaning."

"Yeah."

"You remember that?"

"I remember John cutting into my shoulder."

"I did not see that."

"I could not look away, though he told me to."

"Then what?"

"Then we woke up and had biscuits."

"What were your real parents like?"

"I thought it was a dream," said Bird. "I thought I was going to wake up in the woods again."

"With that thing?"

"Before that, I guess."

"Why were you in the woods?"

"Can't remember."

"What did your parents do?"

"I don't know," said Bird.

"What do you mean?"

Bird was digging at the lichen between the stones, tearing it loose and dropping the small pieces into the mouth of the well.

"I don't mean anything. They were farmers."

"It can be hard to remember," said Mary.

"Yes," said Bird.

✝   ✝   ✝

And then there were those men in the woods. But they were wild. Everything they had, they had with them. No one was looking for them. In fact, Brooke got the sense that they'd done some good by taking them down. Certainly, they'd done what was right for themselves. Any court would see the truth in their claims of self-defense.

There was the scarred Southerner. Something wrong with his face that Brooke couldn't explain. The man had friends. He was well-liked for some reason. Some men just smoothed along throughout life and never really got anyone particularly ruffled in any negative kind of way. Brooke could not remember how they had found themselves at his doorstep. But he had known why they were there. The man had given chase through the living room and out the backdoor in his pajamas. There was a pot of food in the fireplace and a candle burning at the desk. Before setting out after him, Brooke and Sugar had made sure there was nothing much to come home to. They'd done some real damage on the man's home, and stockpiled his weapons on the backs of their horses.

He missed those horses. They never tired before it was time to settle. They didn't make many demands at all. They liked an apple each. His own liked corn. They were agreeable, handsome animals. He did not always get as much as he would have liked of agreeable things.

The man was not a good runner. He was not used to moving in shadows or progressing himself with regularity. His camps were easily spotted, easily tracked, quickly abandoned, and easily destroyed. They, technically, had not killed him. They had followed him around until the corpse revealed itself. He was not a hunter. He did not seem to know the ways of tracking water. It had been Sugar's idea to wait it out and it was a good one. They rode on behind him, kept an eye on him, but did not overtake him. For some time, he had probably assumed he was proceeding well in his evasion. There was some kind of tragedy in that.

When it came to rounding up a hog, Bird was as good a partner as John ever had. The boy was particularly skilled at motivating the pig without startling it. Something in the boy either soothed the creature or hardly registered with it. Either way, it crept along, keeping its distance from the boy but never startling, lashing out, or darting. Bird managed to provoke the pig to the door at the far edge of the pen without ever touching or even reaching out for it. When John's hands fell upon the creature to pluck it out and hang it, the animal seemed as startled as the day it was born.

"You spend much time with hogs?" said John.

"I'm worried it is going to rain," said Bird.

"Rain would be good," said John. "But it won't rain."

"The clouds are all bunched up and thick," said Bird. "The air is all heavy like a sponge."

"Don't get your hopes up," said John.

The drought had been going for nearly two months now. It was getting to the family, cutting into what they could produce for trade. They were scraping by on what the animals brought in. The well was keeping them in enough water to survive and keep the creatures from dying off. But the situation could not hold forever.

"I have made that mistake," said John, carrying the pig like a child across the yard and into the barn. "It's only optimism. There's no harm in it. But it does sting."

He bound the animal's feet and hung them from a small hook overhead. The earth beneath them was dark and hard. He removed a knife from a metal sheet hammered into the wall and began to saw the throat of the pig. It curled its body and tried to swing from him. Or that was how it looked. Either way, it struggled and gurgled and bent against John's grip. Then the animal lost its voice. John held the neck strong and cut deep. It sounded like a thick rope working into an oak tree. Then the sound went hollow and blood fell from John's arms and the pig's throat and the creature began to thrash. John stepped back and the pig spun its body round and round, extending its head as far from its feet as its body would allow, spraying blood along the walls in a circle. On the wall then, Bird noticed there was fresh blood and old blood and stains that were unrecognizable.

Finally, the pig stopped. It centered and the corpse spun steadily on the rope. Then John took it down and carried it to a large iron table at the front of the barn.

"If we got some rain," he said, "things would grow. There would be nothing to be afraid of. We would have more money and more food. It's as simple as that."

John slit the creature from groin to sternum with a thin curving blade. It seemed to bloom slightly, its purpled organs pushing out but not spilling. He pulled them tenderly from the cavity and set them in several buckets behind him. Bird could not recognize the various parts, but they were each glossy, with deep coloring.

"No need to cower in the doorway," said John. "She's as dead as she'll ever be."

Bird was still at the mouth of the barn. He had backed out during the bleeding and was hovering there since. He did not need to advance. The image was grisly and the smell was worse.

"It smells," he said.

"That's iron," said John. "Blood. Entrails. That's food and what makes it food. You'd be better off knowing these things and accepting them. Whether or not you stay with us or take off on your own some day, you'll need to accept what feeds you and what it takes to stay fed."

Bird had not given this the slightest bit of thought. Staying or going. He knew he would not ever go back into the woods. He was suspicious of town.

He stepped into the barn and joined John by the pig. John was working a new smaller knife beneath the skin of the animal and it was lifting away fairly easily. A few white threads like cobwebs clung to the underside and stretched between the skin and the muscle, but John was not forcing anything. It came off more or less like a snake's skin, in several large pieces.

Bird began to tremble. His head went warm and he collapsed. When he woke Martha was at his side. It was evening. He tried to lift each limb to determine if he was bound, but all three rose.

"You fainted," said Martha, "at the sight of a butchered pig."

Bits of the pig came back to him. He pictured it spinning and screaming its low scream.

"John moves fast," she said. She had a small book in her hands, which she closed and set on her lap.

"What time is it?" said Bird. "Am I safe?"

"Of course you're safe, little one," she said. "You've lucked out being found and brought here. There are far worse places to be brought."

"Is John mad?"

"No."

"Why did I faint?"

"Because of all you've been through, would be my guess,"

said Martha. "When John found me, I was mute and uncivil. I cannot reenter my old way of thinking but I remember being fairly terrified of any sounds I might make and the looks they would draw."

"I don't want to faint," said Bird. "I want to be able to help and slaughter pigs."

"There are lots of ways to help aside from gutting animals."

"I want to be able to do what's needed," said Bird.

"There is a variety to our need," said Martha.

"How long does a pig last?"

"For eating, they can last several months. Selling them, they go much more quickly."

"How long does it take to sell one?"

"John traded the bulk of yours this afternoon."

"Then we'll butcher a new one tomorrow," said Bird.

"I think tomorrow you're riding for town," said Martha.

"Why? What if I don't want to go?"

"There's a doctor there who will need to see your wound. And there is trading to be done."

"My wound is fine."

"You're striking an attitude with me, little one. There's no reason for it."

"My name is Bird and I'd like to butcher a pig tomorrow."

"That you're stubborn and proud is all you'll prove by doing so. Do as we need, not just as you like."

She rose and patted him on the head then.

"You are a handsome boy with an eager heart and we are grateful to have you."

✝   ✝   ✝

The water had vanished beneath the sand but Brooke could still follow its coloring. The sand was a bit darker and looser where the stream ran. He could extract the water from the sand using a sock, and carry on. There was no certainty at all in the direction he had chosen. Many towns set themselves up alongside a water source, but not all, and there was no telling what the situation with this water would become. It had already begun to leave him. He was out of wood and keeping warm only by applying his clothes and coat as a poor kind of blanket. It was brutally cold at night and hot during the day. It occurred to him to follow the stream the opposite way, back in the direction from which they came, but he had walked for several days in this direction and doubling back was a hard decision to make.

There was one man among them all who had put up a considerable, worry-worthy fight. Either an ex-soldier or a man with soldierly inclinations. It turned out that his barn was home to a historical armory of sorts, topped off with a cannon and enough balls and powder to give them lasting trouble.

The fighting between them was extensive and this man had the upper hand. It ended, finally, when he bothered with the cannon. Brooke and Sugar were given enough time to approach the barn on horseback. Before the lengthy pause of his wheeling it and gathering the supplies, they had been hiding in the trees, moving about to avoid his rifle fire. He was a miserable shot. At first, they read his pause as their success. They imagined him gunned down and bleeding. They pictured victory. They were cautious in their approach, avoiding the door at the front of the barn and moving quickly past the windows at its sides. How he did not hear them is still a mystery to Brooke. The cannon fired on the trees where they had initially been held up. It cleared a great path, which then surprisingly snapped back into place. A few of the older trees lay stricken, but the younger, thinner ones bent and bent back as if it were a child's game. The barn was filled with smoke then and the noise was of a stunning kind. Ears ringing, Brooke and Sugar broke in through the front door. The man had fallen back from the cannon blow and was discovered by them on his rear in a bit of horse mud. His horses were dead around him as if stricken by a plague. A goat was in the corner, without its mind. They shot the man and butchered the goat. They lived on its meat for the following week.

Soon, the coloring went. Brooke was without a guide or water source. He aligned himself with the sun as if to follow the same direction as before, but there was no way of knowing if the water still ran that way or ran at all. It could have just as easily curved off or died out. He imagined himself sitting on a stool in a bar. There would be some kind of plunky music playing. People laughing indiscriminately. He liked a noisy room. Liked the way a drink would settle in and everything would seem suddenly to pool there in the back of your skull. He shook away the thought when it led to the memory of a bartender they had drowned in a horse bucket just beyond the church steps. They were out of view but the man had made considerable noise. Still, no one had looked between the buildings to discover them. It had been a hasty, unthoughtful act. They had been successful, however, in killing the man and collecting their pay. Brooke realized that much of their success was luck or good fortune or poor decisions gone unpunished. Finally, he had made a poor decision he was paying for. It was no longer about trying to figure who had sent those men after them. It was more than likely the little man who'd razed Jenny's. That was the obvious, easiest thought. It wasn't worth dreaming up other scenarios. But it was now a kind of game he was playing with himself. Something he was interested in seeing out, interested in pursuing, at least until he was no longer in dire straits.

He was torn between the sudden desire to know more about the men and women they'd dealt with, and the simultaneous understanding that they were better at their work for not knowing. Details clogged things up and slowed you down. The more you knew about a person the more complicated it became to shut the light.

He was so horny he would have fucked a hole in the sand if it would have stayed a hole long enough. It was something that came suddenly and strongly. Just like his hunger. It dug into him and made him unreasonable and mean. He did not require much in this life, but what he did require felt to him like pure necessity. He knew he would not die out there in the desert for lack of something to fuck, but it hardly seemed like a life worth living, if he could go on forever like this. He had not given a direct thought to how well set up he was before this mess. He decided that if things were ever again as they had once been, he would appreciate it more: his freedom, his brother, their life on the road and in the woods. What he got to see and experience each day. Most people held up in a small town or on a dried-up farm and each year passed as plainly as the last until a bullet or a fire found you or time just plain ran out. That was not the life for him.

He had had one wife. They were never legally married. She had had one husband before him and it had not ended well. But they were as married as anyone could ever be in all other respects. As it turned out, he was not a good husband. After the first few months, he grew mean. He did not seem to care for her in any kind of regular way. He could feel himself being mean but could find nothing in him that would stop it. He would observe its happening and take stock. *This is a cruel act and those are cruel words*, he would think. And one day she left him for the man she had been married to before. It was out of nowhere that the man arrived and she joined him on his horse, without so much as a goodbye. Brooke had gone in for a bath at the time, but heard the noises of his arrival and her leaving. He pieced it together as he watched them ride away. He was in a towel on the porch as the final moments passed. That man had a quick horse and he had outrun Brooke with little effort. Brooke had chased them south through a desert for three days without ever meeting them, before finally turning back. Then he spent a year drinking and fighting with his horses. They'd shared a small house on a small plot in a small town, and he had four horses and a well to his name. He would gather the horses up and try to knock them out with his bare fists. Mostly they ran from him, but occasionally one would rear up and do him some harm. After more than enough of that, his brother Sugar returned and they started a life together. Brooke was no good keeping still. No good at doing it, and no good when doing it. So they built themselves a reputation for mobile meanness with a professional demeanor. And they'd kept at it until now. He did not know what ultimately became of his ex-wife. He would like to know but would not like to bother finding out.

He was losing his mind. He was chasing down stories and putting one boot in front of the other. There was no water in this direction, no imaginable source of food. He paused a moment then doubled back.

✝   ✝   ✝

Mary was learning to plow. Or, more accurately, she was at her father's side, pulling rocks and shells from the soil and nodding as he spoke to her. He was smiling a lot. He was grinning like a fool. She was running circles around him and chasing insects back into the earth. The plow was an angled wooden thing, dragged by a horse and steered by her father. It was slow work. He looked pleased and determined.

"So Bird just fell?"

"He fainted, Mary."

"Why?"

"He's still healing."

"He's uneven."

"He's unwell."

They were startled then by a sound like thunder.

Bird and Martha were still in the house. Bird spooked at the sound and Martha tried to comfort him, but he climbed under the bed and lay there flat and unlistening. Then the windows began to break. One by one. And the voices of strange men rose up and the wall behind Martha burst into flame. They were burning them out. Bandits, marauders, rustlers, thieves. Hell was finally at their door. Martha retrieved a rifle from the trunk at the base of Bird's bed. Bird inched away from the fire, gathering himself into a little ball. Martha stepped to the window and fired. A thud. A horse's panic. Another shot and then the same.

"Come out, John," a voice said. "It's been long enough, and we are here to collect."

The men moved from view and circled around the house. They were firing but bullets were not striking or passing through the walls. She moved from window to window, watching the front then the back of the house. She caught glimpses of the

101

men, their horses, but they were moving fast, protecting themselves by doing so.

There was a family plot at the top of a well-wooded hill. The field Mary and John were working was a rough halfway point. John instructed Mary to hide with her grandmother, as she liked to do during family games.

"What will happen to you?" she said.

"I will be safe," he said. "These are just men who want money."

"We don't have any," she said.

"I can reason with them," he told her. "Now go."

She ran, stayed low, and vanished into the woods. The sounds of gunfire and horses and voices obscured the hurried footsteps of her leaving. John found a manageable rock and worked his way toward the barn, which was only a few hundred feet from the field and a few hundred more to the house. He was going for his father's rifle and pistol, which he kept with the animals as both a way of honoring the old man and putting him in his place. One of the men turned the corner at the far side of the house and stopped. He was remarkably nondescript. He was dirty. He had hair on his face and wore a hat that shadowed his eyes. He spotted John and John froze.

"John," said the man. "Do you have the money?"

John raised the manageable rock. He looked for any unique features to the man who was aiming the pistol at him. His spurs were rusty, but not remarkably so.

From the window, Martha saw John freeze, raise his arm, then fall. Then she heard the shot. She stepped into the living room and out through the front door where the man who had shot John was turning his horse back to the business at hand. She fired and he fell. She shot the horse as well. It fell upon the rider. Two other men turned back to her after the shot and she fired on them both. One fired his own shot, but it was redirected toward the sky as her bullet landed. The last of them, though she saw him only as the sixth, fired at her from a good distance. The bullet broke the wood of the banister at her left. She walked toward him steadily and he fired again, blasting a hole in the dirt just behind her. He wrangled his horse and tried to still it. She reached what seemed a reasonable distance for her trembling arms, raised the rifle, and placed a bullet in his chest. He received the bullet, hunched forward, dug his heel into the horse's side, and moved past Martha, forcing her back a few steps but not down. She fired several more times but failed to meet the moving target.

Dust held in the air. There were no sounds from outside, only the fire cracking the walls. Bird wet himself and began to cry. He cursed himself and demanded that he get out from under the bed. He told himself again and again, *get out from under the bed*, but he did not move.

The gunshots that echoed throughout the valley sounded almost patient. Inexplicably, the birds in the trees lining the graveyard were still singing. Or chattering. Gossiping. There were no more horses. No more yelling. Just gunshot, gunshot, gunshot. Then nothing but birds. Mary was pacing between the headstones and pulling up dandelions not aligned to a particular plot. She'd pieced together a bouquet. She was not fully ignorant to what was happening, and there was a flood of emotion for each imagined possibility. There was joy and pride at the thought of John rescuing Martha and Bird and the farm, and of them obtaining several new horses to break and befriend. There was sadness and fear for a handful of other, darker, reasons. She kept herself busy and did not allow herself to settle on any particular thought for very long. The birds flitted from tree to tree as if to spread the news of her bravery, her stoicism. She was like a historical person, going up against the difficulties of the world and working to change things through her survival. She had not known this grandmother. She was not a blood relation. Mary set the dandelions on the grave and asked her grandmother what she thought about the whole thing. Her grandmother said nothing, or she blew through the grass and chirped in the trees—Mary hadn't decided how she felt about it. Mostly when she talked to her grandmother, she imagined she was speaking into a well.

Martha grabbed Bird by the wrist and pulled. He yelled stop and reached for the edge of the bed to counter her yanking. No arm rose to meet the impulse and he slid out from under the bed. When he would not stand, Martha dragged him through the doorway, into the living room, and out the front door. She paid no mind to the fire and Bird somehow made it out without a wound. She dragged him through the dirt and over a rock and out to the barn where she finally loosed her grip and released him into the dirt. She had traced an enormous S in the dirt with his back, avoiding the fallen bodies.

"Get up," she said.

Bird turned his belly to the ground. He was crying and could not stop.

"Stand up," said Martha.

He was in the long johns that had once belonged to Mary. He was without footwear.

"Go to the barn," she said. "You'll find John's boots there and a pistol."

The house was burning, nearly half-consumed by flame, and she had no plan or desire to stop it, it seemed.

"They won't fit," he said.

"They'll cover your soles. Now get up."

She scanned the perimeter for anything—another man, Mary. She saw nothing but bodies and a little Bird crying in the dirt.

"Up," she said, "we're moving."

She headed to the barn and got the boots from beside the door. She found the pistol with the rest of the various tools near the back of the barn. She also found a rifle.

When she stepped back out from the barn, she found Bird had hoisted himself into a sitting position.

"I said up," she said.

She gripped him by his armpits. It felt loose and awkward where the stump was, like she was hurting him.

"What are we going to do?" he said.

"We're going to find Mary," she said.

"Where is she?" he said.

"We're going to look for her," she said.

He was up finally. She brushed him off and handed him the boots. They were indeed far too large. They were comically large on him. She nearly grinned when he took his first few steps. He started crying again and she fired a shot into the air with John's pistol.

"No," she said. "Cry all you want once we've got Mary and we've set rangers on those marauders."

"Were they marauders?"

"I don't know."

"Did they take anything? What did they want?"

"It doesn't matter."

"Why?"

"That's not how this works."

"Why?"

He was crying again.

"Because we are always in the wilderness. Beneath everything is the wilderness and there is no end to it."

"What do you mean?"

"You know exactly what I mean, and that is why you're scared."

"Are they going to come back?"

"It doesn't matter."

"Why?"

"Because we won't be here."

They searched for Mary near the well and did not find her. They searched for her in the fields and found only the plow. They followed tracks that led away from the house and into the woods. There were two trails. One led to the cemetery and the other led deeper into the woods and on into town.

"She's in the cemetery," said Martha, "or she's gone."

Bird was kicking stones and dragging his feet behind her. He was no longer really crying but only because he was exhausted and spent. He was dripping pathetically and running at the nose. He knew he had failed in every way you could fail in such a situation. He had been afraid and miserable and had acted as such, which only made him feel more afraid and more miserable.

Mary was kneeling on a grave and arranging dandelions into a cone shape.

Martha lifted her and held her up and examined her. Then she held the girl against her chest and shut her own eyes.

Mary asked what had happened.

Martha did not speak.

Mary asked Bird what had happened.

He was crying, and said nothing.

"We've got to go," said Martha.

"Where is John?" said Mary, because it felt like the right thing to ask.

Sugar's delivery had to be overseen by several of the town's deputies, partially because the doctor had spoken out so strongly against it.

The doctor was a committed drinker. He had steady hands until around 3 o'clock and then he was more than worthless.

Since Sugar's arrival, the doctor had committed himself to enfeeblement. He would sit in the bar and drink, then he would drink in front of the bar, and then he would drink in the alley off to the side of the bar, and all the while he was calling Sugar an abomination and a creature and the devil. He said Sugar was pregnant with his own cock and if he, the doctor, were to squat before him while he was birthing that cock, it would be more or less the same thing as inviting the animal, Sugar, to fuck him.

"I will not be fucked by an animal," insisted the doctor, on a nightly basis. He was a man of medicine. A church-going man. He had survived two wives and had two sons working to keep the peace. He deserved better.

The morning Sugar went into labor, the doctor opened up the bar. The bartender, who lived upstairs in the inn above the bar itself, and who could be blamed to some degree for answering the doctor's insistent pounding at the door, would not take it so far as to serve the doctor at six in the morning. Instead, he suggested that the doctor take lodging upstairs and try to sleep

107

off what was clearly still clinging to him from the night before. The doctor had simply stepped past the bartender, who was in his night cap and pajamas, and had gone around the bar to open the shutters and get the drink himself. The bartender protested but did not make a move to pry loose the doctor's hand. In theory, the doctor was a respected man. He was educated and on the richer side of things and, above all, he was necessary to their way of life. He was not a bad doctor, though he was unreliable. He'd once cured the bartender's ringworm without much fuss, and saved the lives of several men and women who'd come down with some kind of horrible fever just the year before. In theory, he was one of the town's more important men. In practice, he was universally ignored whenever possible.

In the jail, Sugar demanded help but could form no specific requests other than, "Please bring a doctor," or, "Please let me go."

The doctor, drink in hand, held court on the porch of the bar.

"While I've never dealt in creature before this day, I can confidently say that to let this one out early, to open the cell any time within the next three or four hours, would be the same as letting it loose to wreak havoc on the women and children of our good town. A beast like that won't be slowed down by something so casual as labor, at least not until it's well enough along that it's more or less immobilized by the pain and by the position its body will naturally assume."

Four men, one woman, and three children were gathered before him, pausing their daily procession in order to hear more details about what was going on in the jail and why so many deputies were assigned to its security and why the doctor himself had been so put out over the last week. Rumors were spread and the doctor was always talking but something was different about this morning. Curiosities were as bright as the sun breaking over the hills. The doctor rose and swung his bottle like a young girl dancing her doll across the floor.

"We live and see the world progress into strange, dark places," the doctor said. "The stench of what evil is on the horizon is beyond repute. Every morning I wake to the relief that we are still here, that there are familiar faces and friends about me, and then the horror of our situation settles in and I feel both pity and fright. At my life. At our lives. At what's to become of them. We are witnessing the de-evolution of morals into muck. The degradation of decency."

"You're a doctor?" said one of the men. He was sporting a bright white hat and a long button-down shirt tucked into a snug fit of jeans.

"I am THE doctor," said the doctor. "I am the man who would take the bullet from your leg should the rest of the day go rotten for you."

"I appreciate that," said the man, "but right now you're sounding more like a washed-up preacher or a watered-down drunk. Aren't there some kind of preparations to be made?"

The doctor laughed excessively and forcefully. He laughed so hard that a fine mist of spittle glazed those children perched on the steps below him. They wiped their eyes and covered their mouths and crept in closer.

"Of course I'm drunk," said the doctor, "and this ain't spiritual."

"What's the advantage? What's the gain from how you're carrying on?"

"There is none of either. I'm hoping not to gain something, but to lose something."

"Lose what?"

"It's obvious and not worth taking the time to say and you're a fool," said the doctor. "My fear, of course."

The doctor lost his footing for a moment, trying to settle himself back down onto one of the many rocking chairs that lined the wall-length porch of the bar.

"What's to be scared of?"

"The heinous child of two murdering sons of bitches," said the doctor. "The rage of one at learning what he's been through and what he is and the revenge of the other learning what we've done and what we've revealed. We're caught in the middle of two predators, easing their union into the world."

The children were laughing now because the doctor's verve had loosed more spit onto his shirt and thighs. He was a drooling mess and also sweating profusely. He was making no effort to stop or clear his body's leakings.

"They've caught the Dreaded Joneses?" said the woman.

The doctor shook his head, his bottle. "No, no," he said.

"The Upriser Gang? The Broke-Bottlers?" said one of the men.

Again, the doctor shook his head.

"Jack Kraus and Splinter Cogburn?"

"Not them. These are not celebrities. There is no news here, only darkness."

"Who then?"

"Brooke and Sugar," said the doctor.

The small crowd was silent. Then they began to murmur. Finally, one of the men said, "Who?"

"Brooke and Sugar," said the doctor. "Two men who murder. They aren't celebrities. They're *murderers*."

"But we've never heard of them."

"Which makes them all the more terrifying," said the doctor. He darted to grab his bottle as it slipped from his hand, but only thumbed the neck, tipping it as it fell. It broke on the porch but spilled next to nothing, as it was almost entirely empty.

"Seems hardly worth all the fuss," said the woman.

"All those deputies are watching two unknown criminals? With no reputation?"

"One unknown criminal," said the doctor, "but they are not unknown."

"We don't know them."

"You might have had the unpleasant experience of *getting* to know one of them, if we hadn't rounded them up like we did. They are an endless outpouring of wrongdoing. They are a sickness."

"You didn't round them up."

"I was an essential member of the team," said the doctor. "Who has a drink with them? A flask or a dram? I will buy it from you for twice its worth."

The men and women bid their goodbyes without much politeness at all. They had expected a grander reveal. This was all much messier and less exciting than was hoped.

"There's only one?" said a chubby boy at the steps.

"They've been separated," said the doctor. "Not everything is rustling and gunfire. There is an element of planning that can make one's life easier."

"So why all the deputies?" said the same boy.

"Because the devil himself could come tearing out of this murderer," said the doctor. "And his brother's wagon never arrived where it was going. So, caution is the game."

"Are you going to pull a bullet out of him?"

By now, only the children were left, and they were only three:

the chubby boy asking the questions, a pockmarked girl named Alice, with whom the doctor was familiar after last year's pox revival, and the town rascal, Clint. Clint was chewing his fingers and looking restless.

"What they want is for me to deliver whatever he's got inside of him," said the doctor.

"We need more information," said Clint, between bites.

"You'll make yourself sick doing that," said the doctor, "and spread disease. Spit your fingers from your mouth."

"I won't," said Clint.

"Regardless," said the doctor. He rose to fetch more to drink from the bar, but found the door locked and barred.

"You dog," said the doctor to the unyielding oak.

"Is it the appendix?" said the chubby boy.

"A medical man," said the doctor, turning back to the children grandly, drunkenly, with a stutter in his step and sweat on his brow.

"You took out my dad's," said the boy.

"A worthless organ, just waiting to be occupied by this or that malady," said the doctor. "We're sacks of vestigial organs and bones. Most of us is hardly necessary."

He approached the chubby boy then and pinched his gut.

"Ow."

Clint lowered his hand to laugh and lean forward as if he were planning to take part in what was sure to become an ongoing harassment of the chubby boy.

"No, my boy. It is not the appendix."

"What then?" said Alice.

"A baby," said the doctor.

The three children were silent then.

"Did you hear me?" said the doctor.

The chubby boy nodded. Clint cocked his head then looked either way up and down the road. Alice raised her hand.

"Yes, Alice," said the doctor.

"What baby?" she said.

"Sugar is carrying a baby," explained the doctor.

"But…" began the chubby boy.

"It does not seem right, does it?" said the doctor.

"How did the baby live inside him?" said Alice.

"He has all the parts of a woman," said the doctor.

"But he's not…?" said Alice.

"He is not known as such and has never laid claim to the gender," said the doctor.

Clint's open palm met the back of the chubby boy's head then. Clint broke into laughter and took a few steps back as the chubby boy rose to defend himself.

"Don't," said the boy.

Clint nodded, put up his hands, and assured him he would not.

"What does it mean for the baby?" said Alice.

"I don't know," said the doctor.

The clap was even louder this time, when Clint's hand met the back of the other boy's head. So hard was the blow that the boy tipped forward, his palms to the step in front of him, before he was able to gather himself up and chase after Clint.

"Quit it," said the doctor, waving his hand as after a fly.

"I'm confused," said Alice.

"As you should be," said the doctor.

"Is he really a killer?" said Alice.

"Yes," said the doctor, settling into his chair and bringing his hat down to block out the blinding light reflected by the dirt of the road before him.

"Are we safe?" said Alice.

"They would like us to think so," said the doctor.

Across the street, the chubby boy had Clint pinned before a trough full of muck. He was slapping Clint across the face with one hand and scooping muck from the trough with the other. He tipped the muck onto Clint's face, focusing on the mouth, eyes, and ears, and Clint squirmed and squealed, and the other boy's face was like a stone.

When the doctor finally arrived at the jail he had a little girl in tow and was the storming drunk of a man who had managed to keep it going through the night and on into the morning. He pointed to Sugar, who had removed all of his clothing except for his shirt and positioned himself on the bed in his cell with his knees bent, as if napping in a tight spot.

"That," said the doctor, "is crowning."

There were eight deputies scattered throughout the jail's main office, which contained a desk, several chairs, a dusty collage of wanted posters, boxes of bullets, some riding gear, and Sugar's cell at the back.

The deputies appeared confused at the word, but Alice seemed to understand.

"We're deep into it now, deputies," said the doctor.

"We're worried he's dying," said one of the deputies. A young boy. The doctor had seen him around but hardly knew him. He was new to town, flirting with Flora Jean, the gravedigger's daughter. He didn't drink and he didn't chew and he kept to himself in a rather superior sort of way.

"That's because you don't know anything outside of the deputy's game of capturing and killing."

"I served for four years under—"

"You're not helping your case, my boy. Can the cell be

opened?" The doctor's mood had shifted entirely. A kind of excitement came over him when it was time to begin. That, and he was enjoying the fact that Alice had come with him out of curiosity and that she seemed to cling to his every word and movement like a pitch-perfect daughter might.

"Birthing is easy, Alice," explained the doctor, as the young deputy unlocked and cracked the cell's door. "It is a matter of catching. Like waiting at the bottom of a hill to catch a friend who is sledding down it. There's only a small bit of risk. More fun than anything else."

"My mother had seven children and I was the last," said Alice.

"You see?" said the doctor.

"But she passed after I was born."

"Yes, well, birthing seven children is very different than facing the task of raising them."

The doctor sloppily rolled his sleeves.

"I'll need a stool," he reported. The youngest deputy fetched one from behind the sheriff's desk. The other deputies were resigned, reclined, and leaning against this or that. They had done little more than look in the doctor's way since he arrived. Six worthless men and a sheriff, was all the doctor saw. They were as put out by the whole thing as he was, he determined, but weren't doing much of anything about it. A man was not measured by what he did or did not want to do, but how he was able to handle getting through those things he did not want to do. The doctor was a man who liked to make a note when he had a thorough thought, but he found himself without a pen.

"Do you men plan to help secure this child's birth or are you merely hoping for something to go wrong?" said the doctor, addressing the room.

"What child?" said Sugar.

They all turned to watch him. It was as if an object had suddenly come to life.

"You're giving birth," said the doctor.

"How?"

"Through your vagina," said the doctor.

"I do not want it to happen," said Sugar.

"While many things about you chill me to the core, my son, I do pity you right now," said the doctor. "This will be the last easy thing you do, I'm sure of it."

"Bring Brooke," said Sugar.

"Your brother is dead," said the doctor.

Sugar moaned and set his head back. He seemed to instinctively know when to push, and the child was working its way out with little effort or coaching from the doctor.

"Gross," said Alice.

"Yes," said the doctor.

Sugar moaned.

"Is he going to die?" asked the young deputy. He was at the doctor's side then, standing just behind Alice. The sheriff lit a cigarette, and stepped onto the porch.

"I doubt it," said the doctor. "You could get me a basin of clean, warm water. Some soap. Some clean blankets. You could make yourself useful."

The boy did just that. He vanished with a determined air.

"Do you deliver a lot of babies?" said Alice.

"Some," said the doctor.

"Do you like it?"

"Sometimes," said the doctor.

"I am going to die," said Sugar. "But I am not afraid."

"Very good on you," said the doctor.

"Is he going to die?" said Alice.

"They're dirty," said the doctor.

"I…"

"It doesn't matter now," said the doctor. "But you have made a mistake."

"Let me see it," said Sugar. It was chant-like. Less a request and more a rhythm he was holding in his mouth.

Alice brought the baby to his side and knelt to place it in his arms. She showed him how to hold it.

"What is it?" said Sugar.

The doctor set down the dirty, stained blanket and joined the sheriff on the porch. He stuck in a plug of tobacco. His hands were starting to settle. The road was crisp before him and the sun was fully baked in the sky. He needed a drink.

"An abomination," he said, and spat.

Mary, Martha, and Bird had walked through the night. They had not stopped. They had not eaten. Mary spoke as they walked, but of nothing in particular. Bird did not cry. Martha did not respond to the many things there were to respond to, but she watched the edges of the darkness around them and, every once in a while, she would sing. Softly to herself, something Bird could not quite make out. It was not soothing. There was something much worse about it than the silence.

Mary complained that they were not stopping but Martha paid her no mind. Bird was glad to keep moving. He was glad Martha had brought the weapons, hung one from her shoulder and carried one in her hand. They looked natural on her, comfortable, though he had never seen her anywhere near a gun before.

An hour or so after daybreak, they began to see other people.

119

A few men pulling carts along the road at a slow pace. A woman and two children in clean, pressed clothes, carrying small black books held to their chests or under their arms. They were moving toward a thinly populated area. Toward a town that suddenly appeared before them like a mirage.

Sugar was feeding the baby. It was not something he knew how to do, but something that had simply happened to him. It was a familiar enough idea, and when it came time to perform the task himself, something in him settled the child and his own body into place and the baby took hold. The sheriff left the doctor on the porch to smoke and chew and curse and approached Sugar splayed out in the cell with the baby attached. The sheriff gripped the baby by its sides and detached it from Sugar, who protested and was met with the barrel end of peace and order.

"That's enough," explained the sheriff. "You'll hang tomorrow, and we'll be done with all this."

The baby was crying. Screaming. Alice worried they were hurting it and she went out onto the porch to tell the doctor. He was no longer settled there but was ambling back toward the porch where she had first joined him.

When she finally caught up with him, he was at the door of the bar and fumbling to open it against its will. An armed woman and a dirty little girl and a crippled boy were gathered across the street, on the steps of the inn. Alice waved at the boy but he did not notice or he did not care.

"I think it's locked," she said.

"I know it's locked," he replied. "I am *trying* to get in."

"I think they're hurting the baby," she said.

"Babies cry," said the doctor. "That creature will never have a happy life."

"Where did it come from?"

"That's a story for when you're older," said the doctor.

He kicked at the base of the door, knocked with his fist, and pounded with his palm.

There was suddenly a gunshot, and then there were many gunshots. The doctor ducked, then lowered himself onto the porch. Then he rose, grabbed Alice, and lowered the both of them onto the porch. She was crying.

"Are you shot?" she said.

He was not.

He had first thought the shots were a kind of warning from the barkeep to ease off the door, but as they continued he realized they were coming from down the road.

He spied two of the deputies huddled behind a cart and a barrel out in front of the jail.

The windows were broken. He could see the piles of glass shining up from the porch.

"He's shooting from inside," said the doctor.

"Inside of what?" said Alice.

"The jail."

"The sheriff?"

"I highly doubt it," said the doctor.

The bartender cracked the door then and ushered them in. The shots continued. They kept their bodies low.

"Why did they bring this on us?" said the bartender. He kept his hand on the small of Alice's back, pressing her to the floor.

The doctor reached from the floor and batted his hand about the surface of the bar until it found the edges of a bottle. He brought it down and examined the label, then uncorked it with his teeth.

Outside the jail, one deputy reloaded while the other kept his gun on the door. Sugar was moving around inside, but hadn't fired in some time. The sheriff must have been dead. The other deputies were dead. The youngest, their dear friend, was gut shot and slung over the splintered railing that marked off the jail's porch. It bowed toward the earth. At any moment it would come down.

The deputy finished loading and looked to the other from behind his cart. The other deputy was curled up behind his barrel, bravely peeking out every so often to determine what they were up against. They summoned their courage. They spotted the strength in one another's eyes, and the fears. They would stand together. They would avenge their partners and protect this small town. They took their pistols into each hand, gave one another a final look, then rose to rush the doorway.

They moved several crouched steps before Sugar stepped onto the porch and fired upon them. One received bullets to the chest and gut. The other, a bullet to each leg. Scrambling on his back like a beetle, he gathered one of his guns from where it had fallen and brought it up to meet Sugar. Sugar kicked it from the man's hand and sent a stray bullet into the body of the young deputy slung over the porch. The railing rocked with the impact and came cracking, splintering toward the earth, where it deposited the limp body of the young ranger.

Sugar put a boot on the deputy. Sugar was still naked from the waist down. The deputy decided in the brief moment it took for Sugar to arrange himself above him that he would tell the killer everything he wanted to know. When Sugar asked, who are you? who sent you? what's my crime?, the deputy would proudly spill his guts.

"Which way is the desert?" said Sugar, pointing out the various paths leading from town. "Which way the woods?"

The deputy nervously pointed to one path, winding its way past the jail and on out toward a wasteland of red rocks and spiked lizards. Then he thumbed in the direction that lay before Sugar, leading down through the heart of town and back out the other side.

"That way is the woods," he said.

Sugar was loading his pistol.

The deputy could not help but notice that, without his pants, without his unders, this man looked entirely female.

"Thank you," said Sugar. He fired one shot into the eye of the deputy then retreated to the jail to retrieve his clothing.

When the gunshots ceased, Martha worked her way to the window. The three of them, Martha, Mary, and Bird, were on the floor of the inn. The innkeeper had been kind enough to bring them in at the sound of gunfire. When the shots kept up, they took to the ground to avoid stray bullets and being spotted. The innkeeper received an unexpected end after being met with a ricocheted bullet sent through one of the front windows. She was bleeding and propped up against the fireplace, not long for this world.

Against the pleading of Mary, who was clutching Martha's hand and curled up against her body, Martha rose and went to the porch to retrieve her rifle.

The killer emerged from the jail, buckling his belt with a

sinister blankness. He was too far down the main drag to get a good shot, so Martha stepped back in to check on the children.

"The man who killed our savior is out there," explained Martha.

"How do you know?" said Mary.

"How many murderers could be out in this area wreaking havoc at once?" said Martha.

Bird did not hazard to answer that question.

"That is the survivor of those men who shot John," said Martha. "He is still bleeding from the wound I left him with."

"What are you going to do?" said Mary.

"I think I'll wait until he's worked his way down here a bit and try to put one in his back," said Martha.

"That's cowardly," said Mary.

"He's a killer," said Martha. "There's no sense in giving him an opportunity to express himself."

Sugar was rounding up pistols and bullets from the dead men scattered in front of the jail. The rest of the town was shuttered and gathered to the ground.

The sheriff had taken the child somewhere and was vanished now. It was likely he was hiding in an alleyway or behind a box somewhere. He would be waiting for Sugar to make an effort to pass. The safest choice, as far as leaving went, would be to take to the desert. To skip the walk through town and its possible dangers. To take to open territory, with the knowledge that he would be hunted.

But Sugar did not want to die in the desert, without food or water, as a hunted man. He stepped a straight line down the middle of the road, which led through the center of town.

He watched each window as he passed. The first building was shed-like, possibly home to some tools or some dry goods. He couldn't tell from the facade. The bar was next. He saw movement from deep within, but nothing directly at the window. He stepped onto the porch and pulled the hammer back on his pistol.

He opened the door and saw the bar was empty. He heard nose-breathing. Maybe a hand over a mouth. He moved toward the center of the room and then there was a shot from outside.

"Come out," said the sheriff. He was alone, a rifle at his shoulder and a pistol in his hand. "You've had your fun. We've got men posted on the rooftops and we will burn that building down to bring you out."

"Where's the child?" yelled Sugar.

He heard something then from behind the bar and turned slightly to greet it.

"Come out," said the sheriff. "Toss out the guns and come out."

"And what?"

"And nothing," said the sheriff.

Sugar stepped forward and set himself at the edge of the bar's window. The tables around him were still stacked with chairs, as if it were the end of the day. But the door had been unlocked and there was movement from within. So someone was in the room with him, or someones, and they were keeping to themselves, at least for now. He peeked around the edge of the glass and saw the sheriff standing there, alone, his gun held firm on the exterior of the bar.

Sugar examined the bottles lined up behind the bar, checking for reflection.

"Now," said the sheriff.

"Don't think I will," said Sugar.

"We will burn you out," said the sheriff.

"You may do that, but you'll be burning whoever's in here with me."

"Who's in there with you?" said the sheriff. His tone was flat, uncurious.

"Looks like a young child and two old men," said Sugar.

"You're a liar," said the sheriff.

The bartender rose up then, his hands above his head.

"He's not lying, Sheriff," yelled the bartender.

Sugar trained a second gun on him.

"I believe you are in there, Lloyd, but not the child," said the sheriff, from outside.

"You should believe him," said Lloyd.

"Son of a bitch," said the doctor, rising from behind the bar as well. He cast a punitive gaze at his feet then redirected his energy on Sugar.

"There is no child," said the doctor.

"Roy?" said the sheriff.

"Yes," said the doctor.

"It's a little early," said the sheriff.

"Bold words for the only man among the four of us who has failed to perform his job this morning," said the doctor.

"I am doing my job," said the sheriff.

"That's enough," said Sugar. "Bring me the child."

"There is no child," said the doctor.

"I can see her reflection in the glasses," said Sugar.

Alice flinched but did not bring herself up.

"You are mistaken," said the doctor.

"Bring her up and over here now or I will kill you both and fetch her myself."

126

"What's going on in there?" yelled the sheriff.

"He is threatening our lives," said the doctor.

"You are drunk and a fool," said Sugar. "Protect that child's life by bringing it to me now."

The bartender gripped Alice by the arm and lifted her.

"You son of a bitch," said the doctor.

"I do not want to go," said Alice.

The bartender did not speak but dragged her from behind the bar and over to Sugar.

"If I see any more movement in there," said the sheriff, "I am going to open fire."

"You'll kill innocent men or a child," said the doctor, "if you do so."

"Quit moving around, then," yelled the sheriff.

Sugar took Alice into his grip and pulled her against him. He fired on the doctor and brought him down. Alice tried to run but Sugar held strong. He kicked open the door and stepped onto the porch, his gun barrel pressed into Alice's blond hair, singeing it and sending out the most awful-smelling smoke.

"No," she said.

The doctor was fishing for a rifle or weapon beneath the bar.

The sheriff stepped back to account for Sugar's progression.

"Let her go," said the sheriff.

"Where's the baby?" said Sugar. "I want the baby and I will go."

"Well, I did not expect that," said the sheriff, "but you cannot have it."

"Where is it?"

"You'll let her go and then I'll bring you to it," said the sheriff.

"No," said Sugar.

"I'll not have you threaten that girl's life," said the sheriff.

127

"There is no threat if you do as I ask," said Sugar.

"I won't," said the sheriff. "Not as you ask it."

The doctor found a club perched on a row of small hooks hanging under the far end of the bar. He lifted it into his hands and gave it a few limp test swings. It was top-heavy and awkward.

"You will," said Sugar.

Neither man flinched. The mouth of Sugar's pistol barrel was cooling against the head of the child. The sheriff was aiming at the left side of Sugar's chest. It was unprotected by the girl's body, and it was possible he could puncture a lung or even strike the man in the heart if he was steady enough. He pulled the hammer back and ordered Sugar to release the girl.

Sugar did not oblige and so the sheriff exhaled, steadied his hand, shut one eye to aim at Sugar's chest, and fired.

Alice collapsed against Sugar, who stumbled back but did not fall. At first she did not bleed and then she bled profusely from the forehead. The sheriff flinched and Sugar took only a brief look at the girl before firing his counter. The sheriff took two bullets before collapsing to one knee. He raised his pistol and fired again but hit no mark. Sugar, still clutching the limp body of the girl, stepped toward the sheriff and fired again and again as he did so. Bullets ripped at the man who slumped forward onto his bent and planted leg, before tipping over into the dirt. The doctor sprung from the bar then, swinging his club and aiming in a sort of general way at Sugar. Sugar turned and fired on the doctor, but his pistol only impotently clicked at the man who did not slow in his advance. Sugar pulled a third pistol from his belt and fired on the doctor, this time breaking a piece from the club and finally giving the man pause. He was not fully stopped, but he slowed to cast a glance at the mangled club, and this allowed Sugar to plant two more bullets in the bulk of him.

The doctor stumbled but did not fall. The club slipped from his hand and bounced against the road twice, tapping once its top end and once its handle, before settling.

The doctor said, "Stop," and Sugar fired on him again, ending his protest.

There were no men on the rooftops. The town had no response for what had just happened. Things were as still around Sugar as they had ever been. Only, the alleyways were a little safer now. The boxes he would pass, as he went from store to store and house to house, gathering supplies and ending any objections: these were safer too.

Doubling back gained Brooke nothing but a little more time. He soon found the water again, and with it, a few small things to eat. Insects and algae, minnows and tadpoles. He caught a lizard but there was not much meat to it.

There had also been a man in the woods, but Sugar had not known about that. Brooke came upon the man while he was sleeping. Brooke was wandering the woods and discovered a clearing of grass being fed upon by a herd of longhorns. These were burly creatures. He had heard about them and seen their likeness, but had never seen one up close. They were formidable. Their horns were more than long. They were monstrous. The average creature's performed a single curl before branching out away from its face. They split and thinned toward the end as if they were entirely for show, rather than weaponry. They shuttered at his approach but did not resist his hand. He touched one after the other, examining their crunchy fur with his fingertips and saying hello to one after the other. There was a small campfire on the opposite side of the herd and a man on his back with his hat over his face. He must have been sleeping because he did not startle at the sound of Brooke's approach. A man like that was too fit for casual robbery to be ignored. Brooke and Sugar had been in the woods too long for any pretensions toward some code against the act. Codes of conduct were relevant only in the absence of need. Brooke set to the man's nearby bag in search of something that might improve their situation. He found nothing but did wake the man who unsettled his hat and revealed himself to share a likeness with the man who had driven the horse that vanished Brooke's wife.

"It's you," said Brooke.

"I do not know you," said the man.

"This is a faith-inducing level of coincidence," said Brooke.

"We do not know each other," said the man. "I do not know who you think I might be."

Brooke was on the man's throat before he could say much more. The man died quickly and it was no grand affair, but as Brooke sat to his side, reexamining the bag—a little more thoroughly this time—it occurred to him that he did not, in fact, view his wife's true husband as a mortal enemy. He was not really an enemy at all. If anything, Brooke had stolen from the man and the man had only reclaimed what belonged to him. And Brooke had never really gotten along with his wife anyway, so he was no worse for the loss, when he thought it all the way through. The truth was, there was a hostility and a violence in him that was based on no external source. This was not a man Brooke had wanted to kill. Brooke had merely wanted to kill, and there was a man. The herd was too fascinating and dumb to suit the purpose. If the man was who Brooke suspected him to be, there was something meaningful behind the murder, even if there was no real good in it.

He was thinking about it too much. Spending too much time there with the body and the bulls. They had not reacted at all to the killing. The grass was soft and long beneath him. There was a subtle wind around them. This area did not frost, though it was late in the winter months. He and Sugar had taken the route through this part of the plains, feeling that, though a great deal longer, their travels would be more comfortable and they would have a greater chance of staying healthy and fit for when they came out the other end. Brooke found a small kerchief at the bottom of the man's bag. Inside the kerchief was a bundle of small bones held together with a bit of wire. There was absolutely no way of knowing where it had come from or why, but Brooke assumed it was some attempt made by the man to keep his leavings to a minimum. Perhaps these bulls had nothing to do with him and he was on the run. Pursued by men or dogs or men with dogs, and any bit of scent left behind or too boldly displayed would be his undoing. Or maybe he had been traveling with the bulls to best obscure his trail. Or maybe it was an icon of some kind, a bit of religion the man carried with him. Brooke had no religion but knew enough to know that icons were a part of most Sunday gatherings. These manifested in very individual ways in people's private lives and he was no one to judge what a man might carry with him and what it might mean to him. There was a bit of cheese and moldy bread in the bag too, which Brooke pocketed. There were no weapons and nothing more of any use, so Brooke abandoned the bag and the bones and the body and said goodbye to each of the bulls, one after the other.

He loved his brother and they shared nearly everything, but something in him did not want to go into an attempt at explaining what had happened out there in the clearing that morning, so he kept the cheese and bread for himself and left the whole thing unmentioned. That was the one death he carried privately. The one death it was entirely possible no one ever knew he was responsible for, other than himself and the bulls. Whatever happened to the bulls was impossible to say. It was possible whoever had been after the man eventually did catch up with him. They would have been disappointed, seeing their work completed for them, but maybe there would be some condolence in the bulls that were left at their discretion. If he had been the man Brooke suspected, and the news ever made it back to his ex-wife, there was even the chance she would guess it was him who had done the killing. Judging by the man's appearance, he had been out with the herd for some time. Or out in the wilderness for some time. Brooke had not been able to determine the man's route, or had not taken the time to, and it was as possible that he was headed home as it was that he was headed out for good. Either way, if she heard anything she would likely hear that the man had been strangled. And, being a sharp lady and somewhat suspicious, she would likely assume it was Brooke. Which made him happy enough.

At the time, Brooke found it curious that, having had no interest in pursuing them after those first few days, and certainly giving no real thought after that to finding the man and killing him, he had simply stumbled onto the man and into killing him and it was entirely likely his wife would soon hear about it, however many miles away she was and however little she cared to think on Brooke this late in life.

There was no logic to life and no road that could take you straight to elsewhere. Living was all winding around and doubling back. He was walking alongside his old tracks now, watching the stream grow broad and deep again. The red rocks where the wagon sat were even visible far, far off in the distance.

He had no idea how long he had been walking, how many days, how many miles, but knew he was better off now than he had been at the halfway point. He could try to follow the wagon's trail back to the town, at the very least. Maybe the innkeeper would take pity on him. Or had she been setting them up from the very beginning? Had the whole thing been an ambush? How was he to know? How was he to even begin to guess? The stream seemed of an entirely different color than before. Or maybe it didn't. He could not be sure. He tasted it and it tasted like water, but that was no help in determining if the water had somehow changed or if this was in fact the same stream.

They had killed a boy once, but Brooke had not wanted to. Children are stubborn and it is rare that someone else's child will listen to you without being instructed to do so by a guardian. Boys were worse than girls in this regard, and if a young boy got it into his head that you were double-dealing him or treating him poorly, there was no other way of getting around it than to be forceful or to be saved from force by the appearance of the boy's parent. One such boy had caught Brooke and Sugar sleeping on his father's property and had chosen to take the extreme route in addressing the offense. Rifle to collar, he demanded they explain themselves, which they would not be particularly good at doing, in such a position. Firstly, they did not like being threatened. No one did. Secondly, their story was not exactly one to put a frightened boy at ease. They were out to kill someone. Someone who lived in this area and owned a considerable portion of the land. Someone who had a son and a sick wife and a slow-witted brother. Someone whose son was rumored to be a bit of a handful.

† † †

The killer was going from house to house then. Entering, and then shortly after, firing. He was steadily approaching the inn. Martha moved Mary and Bird to the back of the building, into a back bedroom with a large vanity. She opened the vanity, removed the dresses and suits, as well as the bulk of the cobwebs and dust, and instructed them to get in and not to come out, no matter what they heard.

"There are spiders," said Mary.

Martha positioned them beside one another and clipped the vanity shut. She considered turning its front to face the wall, but she hadn't the strength to budge it. She went back to the front room where the innkeeper's body sat slumped. She checked the window and saw nothing. She heard a gunshot, faintly, but did not flinch. She covered the open-eyed gaze of the innkeeper with a bit of lace from the back of the couch. She did not know the name for it or its actual use.

She positioned herself behind the couch and trained the gun at the door. She sat a moment. Listened. She could hear only her heart pulsing in her neck. After a moment of silence it occurred to her that there was no way he wasn't anticipating a gun trained on at least one of these doors he was kicking open. Without a doubt, he would enter prepared for the obvious position she'd taken, and their exchange would be only a matter of speed and accuracy, neither of which did she care to match with someone who'd long been in this line of work.

She examined the room for a better position or plan. The room was only slightly furnished. Two couches facing one another at either side of an empty fireplace. A body leaned against that fireplace, with a bit of lace over its gaze. Across from the body was a low desk with thin legs. It would offer no protection. Behind the desk was a row of small cubbies. They looked something like mail slots but each had been filled with small trinkets, porcelain figurines, and tiny stones or dusty gems.

She heard movement, Mary and the boy shifting in the vanity, banging their elbows and whispering to one another. She heard the vanity's wooden base creak beneath their weight. More gunfire. It was single-sided fire. One or two or three measured shots and then silence. The killer was eliminating the townspeople, one by one. She entered the bedroom in which the vanity was stored and examined the other possible hiding places. There was a closet that would not do. There was space under the bed that would not do. There was the vanity, which was full. And there was a window.

She heard Bird and Mary go silent as she climbed atop the desk.

"Do not step out and do not speak," she said to the vanity.

"Martha?" said Mary's voice.

But she did not reply.

She exited through the window.

In the alley behind the building the town seemed almost peaceful. The dirt there had been smoothed by the wind. Only a few scattered footprints and bits of trash decorated the path. There was a foul smell, but that was to be expected.

She could no longer sense the killer's systematic approach. She spotted a small pile of crates at the far end of the alley, where it opened up onto the town. She kept low and approached the crates for cover. From behind them, she could see the empty street.

The killer appeared then, on the porch of the building across from the inn. She did not know the building's function. She aimed, but it was not a guaranteed shot. She was not terrible with a rifle, but she was not good with a rifle. The killer looked tired, as if he had not slept in days. He was limping, bent slightly at the waist. He looked ill and miserable, like an old dog she and John had once put down together. It was only a puppy. John could not bear to shoot it, so they had carried it in a sack out to the stream near their house and loaded the sack with rocks. The poor thing had not struggled in the slightest. It had even seemed to smile as they crowded the space between the sack and its fur with stones.

She did not like killing things. And here she was, preparing to kill one more thing. Not that she felt conflicted about it. She just didn't like the idea of it, resented that she would carry this weight with her for the rest of her days. It was not a sin, to protect herself against violence by putting an end to it—but the act would stay with her forever. Her mind would always have there to go, that memory to reflect on, and it would likely have a stronger pull than most of the others. Each death did not lessen the load of the previous. But you grew the muscles to better carry them. John used to have nightmares about the men he had killed. He rode with some general during a violent time in the territory. John had said the general's name many times, as if Martha were to recognize it, but she did not recognize it and so it did not stick. John would wake up in the middle of the night sweating and crying like a child. She had not asked, but had assumed he'd done some unforgivable things.

The killer was at the inn, finally. Martha had not raised her rifle, had not even thought to raise her rifle. She had not even registered his approach at first, but snapped into focus when he dumped the spent shells from his pistol and began to reload. They hit the ground like spilled coins. Somehow, the sound of those shells clicking against the dirt rang throughout the town louder than the muffled shots from within each home. It was the sound of him leaving those deaths behind. It was an unnatural sound. It was monstrous. There was a desperate look in his eyes, like a cornered dog. But there was a matter-of-factness to his movement, like a lost man, decidedly looping the same patch of desert land in the hopes that death will find him more quickly. She knew that face. She knew this man. She had been born to kill him.

Just then, Mary appeared in the window from which Martha had exited. She was trying to open it, but could not lift the frame more than an inch or so. She knocked, softly. Martha shook her head. The killer stepped onto the porch. Mary tried again, to lift the window, but with no success. The boy was not with her.

"Martha," whispered Mary.

Martha shook her head, waved her hand.

"There are spiders," said Mary.

Martha waved her hand.

The killer cracked the door and stepped into the inn and Mary vanished from the window.

Martha tried to remember, had she shut the door to the bedroom? She had when she had tried to set herself up in the front room. But after? Before she exited through the window? She could not remember.

There were two windows that looked out onto the alley, the window she had exited from and a window between the alley and the front room. From her position, she would not have been visible from the front room, unless the killer were to press himself directly against the window and look down. From where she was, she had no real view into the inn through either window, and if she rose to one or the other she would expose herself to whomever stood in the room. She kept low and worked her way out from behind the crates and around to the front of the inn. The porch was raised slightly off the ground, but the space between the dirt and the building was not enough for her to squeeze through. A hero would have charged through the front door, but she did not know any heroes. She knew dead men, and the men who'd killed them, and the boy. The killer was inside the inn with Mary and the boy and Mary was out of the vanity. Martha needed to act fast and protect the child, but she was out of any sensible ideas and was starting to feel frozen there on the dirt, hunched beside the front porch. Thinking it through kept her from having to move. She heard no sounds of struggle, no real movement. Every second that passed without gunfire loaded the next with more and more potential. She was bound to break from the weight. She heard wood cracking and imagined the children were done for. She rose onto the porch, flinching at the sound of its creaking, and spotted through the window the image of the killer pulling floorboards up and setting them against the wall. She heard and saw him speaking but could not make out the words. She was perfectly still and silent as she could be. Her breathing seemed too loud and dangerous, so she held her breath. He did not look up. If he had, he would have seen her there on the porch, holding her rifle against her like a rope. Something had happened to her. Time had slowed and she'd lost her nerve. She was as still as a rock or a tree, or a gravestone. He was directing his pistol to the hole in the floor. He was talking and nodding as if to someone who was afraid of him. He shook his head. The door to the bedroom was closed. He reached into the hole and withdrew an infant, wrapped in a filthy blanket. The child was crying and he stood and held it against him. He lifted the blanket to examine its face. He turned and fired into the hole, then tucked his pistol into his belt and headed out the front door.

He saw Martha there, clutching her rifle. She did not raise it. He paused only a moment before directing his attention back to the screaming child, and then rushing down from the porch and toward the stable. Martha had the thought to shoot him in the back, but there was the child. Instead, she rushed into the inn and back to the bedroom, casting only a casual glance at the hole in the floor, the inside of which was too dark to determine much at the speed she was moving. Mary was not in the room. The vanity was shut. She opened it and found the boy hunched, alone, crying into the space between his knees. He had wet himself again, and the floor of the vanity.

"Where is Mary?"

The boy did not speak.

"Mary," said Martha, into the room.

There she was, under the bed. Her hands appeared first and then her face. She did not seem upset, but was glad instead for Martha's return.

"There were spiders in the closet," she said.

Martha scooped her up. She would have scooped the boy up too, but for the urine.

"Stay here one more second," she said to Mary.

"I don't want to go in the closet," said Mary.

"Just sit on the bed then," said Martha.

Martha set her hand on the back of the boy's head. She told him it was okay and that they were safe. He seemed comforted.

"I was scared," he said, and she told him it was okay.

She left them, the boy in the vanity and Mary on the bed, and returned to the hole in the floor of the front room. Inside, she was able to make out a man on his back. There was a bit of light from the room and the cracks in the floor and she could see that he was on his back and still. A dead man. He had on the clothes of a mobile man, a deputy or a rancher, not a retail man or a smith or an innkeeper. She could not see his face.

"Is there anyone alive in this hole?" she said.

There was no reply.

A horse thundered past the inn then and she spotted the killer on its back, vanishing toward the path that led to the woods. He was not hunched over or working the horse for speed, but was instead upright and gentle looking. She determined he was still carrying the child. It was hardly larger than a bowl, that child. She could not imagine what a man like that would want from something so small. She assumed it was the baby of a landowner or a political figure, and that he was holding the baby for ransom. But there was always the possibility that the man was evil incarnate and that the things he was determined to do with that baby would not reward imagining.

"Mary," said Martha. "Do you remember how to make a chicken?"

"Yes!" said Mary. "You pull out all the feathers and bake it in butter."

"Do you remember how to kill a chicken?"

She did not.

"It is not hard," said Martha.

"Is it like killing a hog?" said the boy. He stepped from the vanity.

"We need to strip you," said Martha, and she did just that. He resisted only slightly as she undressed him and set to the drawers for something to cover him with.

"It is much like killing a hog," said Martha. "It is easier, in fact."

"Are we going to kill and make a chicken?" said Mary.

"Two doors down," explained Martha, "you will find a pen with chickens in it. You will find grain for those chickens and you will find horses and maybe a hog or two. I cannot guess at everything and I did not see everything. Here."

She handed a small dress and an old tattered button-down to the boy.

"This is all that will hold to you," she said.

"We'll need a knife to kill a hog," said the boy, wiping his face and pulling on the clothes as Martha handed them over.

"You will find a knife in the kitchen of the building across from us. That is where the stove is and the pots are. I spied the layout through the window. Everything you need is there."

The boy was dressed. Mary was excited for the chicken.

"Are we safe?" said Mary.

"Yes," said Martha.

"Is it over?" said the boy.

"No," said Martha. "When I'm gone you'll have to kill and cook the chickens yourself. You will need to keep yourselves hidden and protected. Do you know how to fire a pistol?"

They did not.

She showed them how to pull the hammer back, point, and told them to squeeze the trigger firmly.

"It is not a difficult thing to do," said Martha, "firing a gun. But you will find it difficult to hit your mark at first and I recommend you practice."

"Show us," said Mary.

"I am leaving," said Martha.

"Where are you going?" said the boy.

"After that man," said Martha.

"Why?" asked the children.

141

"Because he has taken a child and he was the man who killed your father, Mary."

"John was not my father."

"Yes, he was," said Martha. "He raised you. He was a father to you. He made us a home. He was a good man who did not cross lines. He should be avenged."

"How do you know it was that man?" said Mary.

"I feel it," said Martha.

"Don't go," said the boy.

"I am going," said Martha. "You will do as fine without me as you did with me."

"It's not true," said Mary.

"What is a venge?" said the boy.

"Stay hidden," said Martha, "and keep yourselves protected."

To this day, Brooke did not know why his brother returned when he did. He'd had no reason to. Their business was finished and they had not had much love for one another growing up, outside of the unavoidable amount that came with the need to know yourself a little better and have some camaraderie over the miseries of your particular childhood. It goes without saying that their father was a rough man. They had not known their mother. From Brooke's earliest memory, Sugar had been a boy and their father had treated him as such. It was not until they were old enough to ride horses and kill snakes with traps that Brooke identified Sugar's body as being different from his own. And it was only a short while later that he began to develop an urge toward those differences. They had a white room. A cluttered white room that was used for no particular purpose other than storage. It held the sunlight like a lamp. The windows sagged and spiders hung in the panes. Sugar was gentle then, but his father took that from them. Their father toughened both of the boys until they were mean and capable. To the best of Brooke's knowledge, that man was Sugar's first. Brooke had found them in that cluttered white room. Everything had some bit of the man's blood on it. Every object in the room announced what the boy had done and that they were now alone and without a plan for how to proceed. There was a knife in Sugar's hand and he was crying. His hand was as thickly covered as the blade it held. They buried their father where they buried men and women who wandered beyond their fence, just beneath the apple trees behind the house. It was a fertile yard. They had not cleaned the white room but had sealed it off and let it stand. Years passed. They knew how to farm. They knew how to trade. They made do. Most people did not ask about their father. He was not well liked. One man came asking, claiming the man owed him some money for a pony the boys did not know, and had heard nothing of. It seemed like a lie. A pony. What use would their father have for a single pony? Men were always talking to them about ponies, as if it were the only thing boys knew or had any interest in. Sugar had gone wild at this point, and would scream until whatever it was that was setting him off changed in some way. Sugar set to screaming at the man who came asking about the money for the pony and Sugar moved the man down the hill and down the road with the screaming he did. The man protested and tried to stand strong but there was something wild and frightening about Sugar in that mood and it would have taken a very strong and confident person to stand against him. This man was too full of flinches. He did not come back after he was finally gone. One night, years into their life together on the farm, for no obvious reason, Sugar showed Brooke what their father had liked to do to him. They got along, the brothers. They worked in equal measure. Their days were not particularly difficult to get through. There was no purpose to any of what they were doing outside of getting it done and having enough to do it all again the next day. They lived like lizards. Or the way apples keep coming back and falling to the earth. They sat on the porch sometimes and drank grain alcohol and did not say much. When they did what their father had liked to do, Brooke sometimes worried that Sugar would kill him. He would vow never to do it again. But he always did it again, whenever the urge came—which was fairly regular—until the day the barn burned and they lost their house. They lost their minds a bit that night too. There was no way of knowing how the fire started. A lamp in the barn, maybe, and a cow or a fox or a gust of wind. It didn't matter. It mattered that the house lit and the fire spread and it was dry and had been dry and everything had just been begging to burn. They took two horses and rode to town. There was no fire there. So they went back and brought some of it to town with them. Torches made out of tools from the barn. They were not good boys. They were on the cusp of becoming not good men. It was a small town and the people had not expected the kind of evil every man is capable of, if he has a partner and the right state of mind. They brought the town down around them as the fire had brought down their barn and their home and any claims they had to a legacy or permanence. People died, but Brooke did not know how many people. More than he could think to count, it was likely. They screamed and came spilling out of the buildings. One man was diligent enough with the well and bucket to keep the fire from spreading to his front porch for a time. There were houses scattered in the countryside that bled out from the edges of the town, but Brooke and Sugar did not bother with the glut. There had been no plan and they were not clinical in their state, so they finished the edges of what they'd started and left the town for the wilderness. They rode for several days before Sugar split. It had been at least two since they could last smell the smoke. Sugar made whatever kind of noise he wanted packing his bag and saddling his horse, but offered no farewell or any other proper acknowledgment of what was soon to pass between them. Still, there was no attempt to hide his actions or intent. Rather than rising to join him or chase after him or even demand that he explain himself, Brooke had simply watched his brother go and figured that was the end of it. When Sugar finally returned years later—much in the fashion that he had left—Brooke only noticed one discernible difference. Sugar didn't scream anymore.

And Martha left. They called after her but she did not flinch. She found a gelding in the same stable the killer had pulled from. She was not a fan of bareback but had no time for saddling. She nudged the horse's shoulders, delicately directing him over to a crate that would give her the height she needed to mount him with little additional effort. She took the ride slowly at first, letting the horse get a sense of her body and getting her own sense of the way the horse would respond when she shifted her weight. She was not experienced, but the horse was understanding and patient. After a few moments, she dug in and set off down the path in pursuit of the killer.

The baby would not stop crying. Sugar did not know what to do or where to go because he did not know the territory. Here, the trees were shorter than the ones he'd known, thicker and closer together. You could not ride fast through these woods. They were heading higher and higher up between the mountain ridges on either side. It was getting colder. There was a body hanging from a tree overhead and Sugar passed beneath it slowly. He did not recognize the clothing or the man. He felt then that this was what they had planned for him all along. There would be no ceremony to his end. He held the baby against him and tried to warm it. He could make out faint ruts hardened into the dirt, and he tried his best to follow them. It would not hurt him to linger outside a populated area, though he would need to establish a safe distance. His mind was not working as it normally did. He could not focus with the child crying. He was overrun with thoughts unrelated to the matters at hand.

He made a hard plan to stick to the ruts and see where they took him. It would make it easier for anyone following him to track him, but they would not be after him for at least half a day, if not more. It was entirely possible he had taken out every living thing in that town, other than the horses and the hogs and the chickens. He had been merciless. There was something divine to it, but he did not feel elevated. He felt more self-assured. Brooke was dead and he was alone with this child. Sugar thought that maybe if Brooke was here he would feel less conflicted about leaving the child or drowning the child and riding on. As it was, something was keeping the thing pressed to his chest. Something made him want to warm it and stop it from crying. He did not feel a tenderness toward it, but felt a strong desire to balance it out. To put the creature and himself on a more even keel.

When night fell, he did not stop riding. The baby cried as if that were its only function. It cried as a healthy man might breathe. It was a sound he found impossible to ignore. When

146

the stars were out, Sugar slowed to a trot and tried to feed the baby. He had some cheese in his front pocket, and a bit of bread in the other, and he pressed small chunks of each to the baby's lips, but it would not accept them. The bread gummed up there and broke apart and the baby cried and sent the little balls down its neck or onto the back of Sugar's hand. The horse seemed tired. He was huffing and lagging. Sugar was tired. The baby was crying and, maybe, Sugar hoped, tired. They could not sleep until something in the landscape changed, until they were more hidden. Sugar remembered then where he had held the infant the moment after it was born. He opened his shirt and held the baby at his chest. The baby gummed about for a minute then took hold. It was painful, but ignorable. The minor irritation was far preferable to the crying. Sugar realized suddenly how quiet this particular wood was. The baby was working his chest and Sugar held it and rode slowly between the stubby trees. They needed to take it slow anyway because there was no moonlight and Sugar could see only a foot or so ahead of them at a time. The baby went on like that. It hurt a little more as the time passed but Sugar thought of other things and let the pain melt into his other concerns.

He did not so much care who had been after them, who had caught them, now that he had worked that town over and felt as safe as he ever could feel. He did not prefer to ponder the mystery of what had happened, but instead preferred to set himself up somewhere for a bit and try to get a few good meals in and a few good nights' sleep. He was long overdue for a bath and a fizzy drink. These had been his simple desires what felt like only a day or two ago. It had been much longer, but the events did not come together in a way that suggested the passing of time. Rather, his memory of the past few days was scattershot and rough. There was a lot of hurry to it all. The baby gagged and spit fluid onto Sugar's chest, then settled back into Sugar's bent arm. Sugar did up his shirt then dug his heel into the horse's side. They trundled along only briefly before the child burped and fell to something like sleep.

The storeroom beneath the kitchen was full of jars and sacks of food and smelled like clay. It was cool and pleasant to stand in.

"We might never have to kill a chicken," said Mary.

Bird held a jar between his knees and pried loose the lid. He let it fall to the floor, then set the open jar on a shelf and ate the jam inside with his fingers.

"I would not mind doing it," said Bird.

"But it would maybe be hard and chickens are tricky," said Mary. She read the labels on the sacks one by one. "Flour, grain, oats, flour, flour, salt, flour. This little one is yeast. We can make a bread."

"How?"

"With these things and the oven," said Mary. "We used to make bread every week. You just mix these things."

"How long before these things are bread?"

"Not long," said Mary. "Once everything's in order."

"I'd like to eat hot bread," said Bird.

"Do you think we are the only people left here?" said Mary.

"I hope we are the only people left here," said Bird.

"I would be sad."

"It's safer that way," said Bird.

"People aren't bad," said Mary.

"Bad ones are bad," said Bird.

"Were you scared earlier?"

"You just mix these three?" said Bird.

"And water," said Mary.

"Where's the water?"

"I don't know," said Mary. "That's why we need to find more stuff first."

"Fine," said Bird. "Do you think Martha will come back?"

"Yes," said Mary. "When she's done. She is very dependable."

"She's going to kill that man?"

"I don't know."

"I hope she does," said Bird.

"Why?"

"Because it seems like the right thing and I would feel safer and better."

"You have little faith in people."

"I guess," said Bird.

"I hate to see anyone put to death," said Mary.

"That's foolish," said Bird.

"Why?"

"Because the only way to deal with an evil thing is to put an end to it."

"I don't like it as an idea," said Mary. "I won't agree to it, but I will not be called foolish."

"Then let's concern ourselves with bread," said Bird.

The building had three stories: two bedrooms in the upstairs and a hallway with a ledger and a cash register. Beneath the floor level, where the restaurant was and the tables and chairs, there was the storeroom. In the rooms upstairs, they discovered warm clothes, blankets, and a basket full of buttons of various sizes. There was also thread in a drawer and several cans of oil for the lamps.

There was a long jacket hung from a peg by the door that

led to the kitchen. There was nothing in its pockets. They could work the stove well enough. They could keep the fire going with wood from an enormous stack behind the building.

Every now and then, Bird would check the windows. He saw no one and nothing moving but the few remaining horses.

"What if he comes back?" said Mary.

"That's why we have the pistol," said Bird.

They took the pistol out behind the building. A hundred or so feet away, there was a wagon. They flipped it over and set a milk bottle on it. They walked away until they were a distance they could be proud of.

"I would like never to shoot a man," said Mary, "but I can shoot bottles for sport."

"How many bullets do we have?"

"She said we could find more, if we looked."

"All we found was buttons and a coat."

"I think she meant... around." Mary pointed to the backs of the adjacent buildings. She swept her hand from left to right.

"She said to stay hidden."

"I think we're meant to sneak," said Mary.

Bird pulled the hammer back on the pistol. The pistol was heavy enough to make him feel off balance, as if he were listing in its direction and would topple over without serious concentration when he fired. He held up the gun and exhaled. He squeezed the trigger and the gun flew from his hand. The floor of the alley coughed dirt several feet to the left of the wagon.

"You are our protection?" said Mary.

"It's not easy," said Bird.

Mary took the pistol and fired without much hesitation. She splintered the wagon a few inches from the base of the jar.

"We cannot shoot," said Mary. "But I'm better."

"We have to practice," said Bird.

"You can practice," said Mary, "once you've found more bullets."

Mary made bread and Bird caught and killed a chicken. They kept quiet and did not explore much outside of the building with the kitchen and the bedrooms and the storeroom—and no one else, if they were around, made themselves known. There was butter in the storeroom, for the bread, and lard to cook the chicken in. They salted everything heavily. They found wine under the counter and tried it and did not like it. There was a fireplace near the base of the stairs and they made a small fire, more for entertainment than out of necessity. They did not sleep well. They made pallets on the floor near the fire with the blankets from upstairs and the clothes from the trunks. It went unsaid but understood that upstairs would not have been a comfortable place for either of them to spend the night.

Bird kept the gun near his pillow. He watched the fire in its metal. He had not wanted to become a gunfighter but it seemed like he was going to have to become a gunfighter. Mary did not have the follow-through for it, even if she was a better shot.

"Please stop staring at the gun," said Mary.

"I'm thinking," said Bird.

"About the gun?" said Mary.

"About having to use the gun some day."

"It is thinking like that that will make it so," said Mary.

"That's foolish," said Bird.

"You are an orphan who doesn't have the capacity for reason or high thinking. In his whole life my father never once drew his gun."

"And he was murdered," said Bird.

"You're frightening me and making me feel alone," said Mary. "You are supposed to be my little brother."

"I am not little."

"You are a cripple."

"I'm not a cripple."

"I do not want our friendship to go on like this. You need to think of something else to talk about and think about other than guns and killing and dying. I won't have any more of it."

"You sound like Martha used to sound," said Bird.

They were silent for some time. Mary might have slept. Finally, Bird said, "I am glad you're here."

Mary did not respond, but she shifted, eyes closed, to face either him or the fire.

In the morning, they were friendly again. They all but finished the bread, then gathered small rocks from behind the building. They sat, leaned against the building, and took turns trying to throw the rocks into a bowl they had set a few feet away from them.

At first, neither could do any more than hit the side of the bowl and scoot it an inch or so in either direction. After some time, they started landing the rocks in its center. Bird landed four in a row then turned to Mary and said, "I would like to go into the other houses and find bullets for the gun."

"It makes no difference to me," she said, "but it is not a path I would pursue."

"I don't know what we're to do here," said Bird.

"We can do anything we like," said Mary. "We are on our own now."

"I don't know what that means," said Bird.

"It does not mean anything," said Mary. She tossed her last rock at the bowl and it ricocheted off the side.

"I have a scared feeling," said Bird, "and I cannot get rid of it."

Martha watched the killer make a modest camp. From a low hill, she could make out his shadow and then, with the light of his fire, his face and the baby in his arms. He held the baby's face beneath his jacket, and he rocked it for several minutes. Then he set it to sleep on a pile. She watched him pick at the fire and set his heels by its outer coals. She worried that he would look up toward the night sky and see her outline on the horizon, or that he would be able to hear her breath working its way down the hill and into the branches of the trees above him. She seemed to be breathing abnormally. Snorting like a beast. Heaving like her father in the throes of a coughing fit.

The killer did not sleep, but picked at the fire whenever his head began to drop, or wandered the small circle of his camp. He did not smoke. He did not sing or talk to himself. He was still up until the moments bordering sleep, and then he moved just enough to keep it from overtaking him. Or so it seemed from her vantage. She studied him and tried to know him well enough to make a plan. He was like a fox in its den, or a snake in its pit. She wished she was truly a sharpshooter, able to pick him off safely from a distance. She did not think she could surprise him. She was not a faster draw. If it came to a fight, she would not be victorious. There was a chance she could outride him, seeing as she was only one, and he and the child were two. She slid herself back down the hill and out of view. Her horse was tied up, shadowed by a cluster of thin trees, but still visible if one were to happen upon them. She made herself flat against the dark hill.

During the night, birds settled on either side of her and picked at the hill for insects or seed. She was still and they moved over her and around her indifferently. They were focused on their task. They squeaked, but seemed to communicate nothing. She felt pity for them that they had no higher calling. But there was something simple and direct about the way they lived, and that was admirable. She turned over and crawled a few feet on her belly, scattering the birds. She pointed her right elbow into the dirt and positioned the rifle against her upturned palm and its corresponding collar pocket. She fired and hit the dirt between the fire and the man. He was up then and headed for cover, but she managed two more shots that sent him sliding into the dirt. She was astonished and proud. Each shot had felt less natural than the previous and she had become convinced she was incorrect in her decision to open fire from a distance, rather than to overtake him on the path. But it had worked. There it was. He was slain.

She hurried down the hill, leaving the gelding tied on its opposite side, along with her things. She came upon the body and fired several more shots into its hulk, splitting his leathers and spitting blood onto her leggings and thin-soled shoes. She winced. The baby was screaming unlike any child she had heard before. She lifted it and tried to settle it by whispering sweet things and bouncing it, but nothing worked. She dug through the killer's belongings and could not find much of use. The food was far from edible and his weapons or tools were crude and few. She took a blanket for the baby and investigated the corpse's pockets. Again, nothing.

She carried the screaming baby back over the hill to her horse. Snow began to fall. It had hardly felt cold enough for snow before, but there it was, drifting along like ash at the edge of the world.

154

She held the baby close to her chest as she pulled herself onto
the horse. She had no milk to offer the child, nothing to warm it
other than the blanket, so she undid her blouse and positioned
the baby directly against the warmth of her body. She did up
what she could of her shirt over the baby and wrapped herself in the blanket. Again and again, the baby took hold of her
nipple and tried to wrench life from it. Nothing came. It was
painful, but she let the baby work at her, as much as she could
stand it. It was the least she could do. She rode slowly, trying to
trace the route they had taken from the town where the boy and
Mary were waiting.

Soon, though, the path was indistinguishable. A thin blanket of snow covered every inch of ground, and weighted the
branches of the fir trees that seemed to go on endlessly in every
direction. She fired her rifle into the air and the baby screamed,
but otherwise would not let up.

Then there was a whole slew of men Brooke had killed for
what most would call honorable reasons. He wandered a bit
after Sugar left, without a home or a town to call his own. He
had no friends and no sense of needing any. He needed food
and reasons to stay upon his horse, which were running out
as he came upon more and more miles of nothing. Finally, he
crossed paths with a group of men celebrating a recent victory
over a team of bandits riding north, looting small towns along
the way. They had slain the bandits, returned a percentage of
their loot, and were now celebrating in the woods. They liked
to drink and sing and Brooke soon learned that he too liked
those things. He spent the night with them—they were merry
enough to accept him as one of their own, knowing nothing

about him, where he'd come from or where he was going. Soon, though, he learned that this militia was made entirely of men looking to blur their pasts. They rode nameless and unadorned. They relied on no one outside of the group, and were slow to trust on less celebratory occasions. They had their fair share of inner turmoil, but it was repeatedly squelched by an unspoken understanding that the whole thing only worked if they worked together. As soon as they turned against one another they would be back on their own again. For these particular men, the fear of that was enough to keep them riding quiet, day to day.

During that time, Brooke must have killed fifty men. Maybe a hundred. He did not remember the majority. They often tracked and killed one man at a time. Rapists and murderers. Plenty of bandits. It was more than likely they killed a large portion of innocent men. If any man felt guilt about that, he did not make it known. Brooke found himself pleasantly at ease with following the instruction of a posted sign, or a desperate sheriff, or even consistent word of mouth.

In between hunts, they would drink. Some of the men had wives and children, or mothers, sisters, brothers, fathers, cousins, grandparents who depended on them. Some of them would send home money. A few even wrote letters. No one talked much about their personal lives. None seemed too satisfied with the hand life had dealt them.

They played cards sometimes, late into the night. They were not emotional drinkers. There were not many physical altercations amongst the men, and few wept or carried on, as Brooke would later witness over and over at card games in nearly every town he occupied for more than a few nights. When they played, these men were a casual kind of serious. They took each hand as it came and played and bristled slightly at a loss, but it rarely went any farther than that.

One man, an older one who called himself Grot because he "liked its sound," used to sing the loudest at night and throughout their daily rides as well. His hair was long and gray and he wore a beard. The backs of his hands were crisscrossed with scars he'd likely dug himself. He shot animals from his horse throughout the day, for sport. Deer, squirrel, pheasant, lizard. But he did not collect them. Sometimes, another rider would, and he would laugh at them or ignore it. It was bothersome, but not unforgivable. One night, he lost his temper over a few pieces of gold and sprung on the boy who'd won them. Simple things seemed to bring out the worst in people. He plunged his thumbs into the boy's eye sockets and scoured the sight from them. As the boy lay there screaming and clutching at his face, Grot lifted the boy's beer in a bloodied hand and drank what was left of it. He struck the boy then with the empty bottle, shattering it and silencing him. He seemed to relax then. The other men around the fire rose and wrestled him up and over to a nearby tree. He managed a few blows across the necks and faces of these men but nothing that slowed them. They hung him and watched him kick and when he was done, they shot and buried the blinded boy.

That was the way of things. They were men without a country, but each individual answered to the group. Brooke did not ask many questions, and enjoyed well enough their day to day to keep in line with what they seemed to expect of him. They sang a number of songs, but Brooke's favorite was the simple one. On and on as they rode, or as they sat together and drank late into the night, they would sing:

Drink and Hang
and Drink and Hang
and Drink and Hang
and Drink and Hang
On and on until it slowly, imperceptibly shifted to:

Drinking, Hanging
Drinking, Hanging
Drinking, Hanging
Drinking, Hanging

But it was all a mess now, thinking back on it. It could just as easily have been a decade with these men as a week. His memories were insubstantial fragments standing in for a much larger whole. Like how a wedding ring is said to represent a marriage. Or an old soup bowl in the dirt, a way of life.

Bird was dragging the bodies into the middle of the street and lining them up. Mary woke on her pallet and found the room empty, but for the chairs and the dishes from the night before. She heard the dragging sounds and, from time to time, the strained clap of a swinging door. She crawled to the window and peeked out and there he was, hunched and gripping an older man by his red pajama shoulders, dragging him with one arm through the dirt toward the center of the street. Some of the bodies had thin little lines of blood twisting up to them. Others had a body's width of displaced earth tracing their path, as if they'd crawled from their front porch and down into the middle of the street to flip onto their backs and bask in the sun. They were cooking there in the unbroken heat. But they were not sweating.

"I cannot imagine what it is you think you're doing," she tried to say quietly from behind the door.

Bird did not respond, but instead settled the man a foot or so from a medium-waisted woman in a frilled blue and white dress.

"What are you doing?" she said, a little louder this time.

Again, Bird did not respond, but settled the man and turned back toward the home from which he'd drawn him.

"Bird!" said Mary. She stepped onto the porch of their home and checked either direction, up the street. "Stop."

Finally, Bird turned.

"They're all dead, Mary. Everyone here."

"I know," said Mary.

"How did you know?"

"That man was killing them."

"But they're all dead. Every single one of them. He killed every single one."

"I know."

"We are living in a town full of bodies."

"Don't touch them."

"Look at all of them."

There were all of the deputies, in a line. Then several men and women of middle age or older, and two boys who might have been fourteen or so. A young girl, probably thirteen. She had been bleeding from the waist before she died. Another girl had bled from a wound in her forehead. Her eyes were open and staring and they held the pale blue coloring of the thin clouds above her.

"I don't want to," said Mary.

"Well, you have to," said Bird.

He turned and moved steadily toward the next home in the row that lined the backbone of this small town. He entered and the door swung shut behind him.

Mary went back into the building with the kitchen and she grabbed two plates from the table. She came back outside and when Bird finally emerged with a fresh body, another boy, this one just slightly younger than the rest, she whipped the first plate at him and struck him in the hand.

"Ow." He dropped the body and turned and she moved closer and whipped another plate at him.

"Stop," she yelled. "Stop, stop, stop," as if she were whipping an endless supply of plates at him, but she was only spinning her hands out in front of her and screaming.

"I can't," he said.

"You have to," she said. "I do not want to see them."

"You have to," he said. "We have to do something with them. We can't leave them stuck up in their houses like this. They're rotting on their dinner tables. They've wound up in the most horrible arrangements." He was crying and gripping the young corpse again. This time, Mary let him drag it past.

She would not help him move the bodies. Instead, she agreed to dig. Finding a shovel wasn't hard. She took the smallest and newest looking one and set to digging a few hundred feet from the stables at the far edge of town. Beyond that, there was only desert. A sun, all but risen. Looming red rocks like giants coming to crush them for all the damage they'd done.

She was not able to dig very much of the hole at all before a break was necessary. It was hardly big enough to bury a hand. She'd brought the wine out with her, some of the bread, and a chicken leg. She did not want to go back down that road any more times than was absolutely necessary. She did not like the wine but drank it down because she knew that it was supposed to be good for upset feelings and stomach trouble. She'd already had to dig several small latrine holes, in addition to the large one she was working on. She felt like something was eating away at her insides. She did not enjoy the idea of eating, but knew she needed to. It would be the first bit of food she'd managed all day, and she was working hard and needed the strength. To get the wine down, she held her breath, took it into her mouth, then swallowed hard and fast. Then she shoved a chunk of bread into her mouth to sop up the taste. She followed that up with a bit of chicken and the taste was nearly gone. The wine was unpleasant and burned in her gut. But it was settling her a little. She noticed that when she turned her head, it took a moment for her to realize she was looking back at those rocks in the distance. Each new vision took a moment to snap into place. It was a decent feeling, but she did not exactly like it.

"You have not finished even one hole," said Bird.

She'd seen him coming, but had not lifted herself from the dirt to take up the shovel.

"It is hard to dig a hole the size of a body, and you want me to dig twelve."

"Fifteen," said Bird.

"But I don't even want to dig twelve."

"You've got to, Mary."

"I need help."

"But you won't help me move them."

"So dig with me then move them and I will go to bed. I can't stand today and I can't stand what you have done."

"What have I done?"

"You have made this place horrible and made me feel frightened and taken away my sense of security in our building with the kitchen while we wait for Martha."

"Martha is not coming back."

"Yes, she is."

"That man killed everyone, Mary."

"So?"

"Not one of them survived."

"Stop it, Bird. We survived."

"Because we were hidden," he said.

"I've been looking," he said, "and I've found no one."

"I cannot dig fifteen holes," said Mary.

"Then I will dig them," said Bird.

He took the shovel from where she'd set it and he bent toward the small hole she'd started. She drank more of the wine. He plunged the shovel into the dirt and leveraged it against a bent leg to extract the shovelfull. Again and again, slowly, he unearthed handfuls of dirt. A considerable amount was lost back into the hole, but he kept at it and it began to make a distinguishable difference.

After an hour or so, he had nearly completed a hole long enough to set a body in, but far too shallow for it to stay set. Mary was still to the side of the grave. The chicken and bread were gone. The wine too. She was alternating between sitting and watching and resting on her back to stare at the clouds moving past.

"You could get a second shovel," said Bird.

She lifted her palms and showed him that they were spotted with blisters.

He lifted his palm and showed her the same.

"We cannot dig fifteen holes," she said.

He nodded. He was sweating and sore and there were still more houses to check, more horrors to discover.

"We could dig one big hole," he said. "We could put them all together."

Mary liked it. Both as an idea, the whole town together like that, and because it meant the level of the digging left to do was greatly reduced.

Bird found her a second shovel and they set to widening the hole. She wrapped her hands in the hem of her dress. Bird removed his shirt and wrapped his wounded palm in it. It was already bleeding slightly, and it stained the shirt as he worked. He seemed less and less present to Mary. More and more focused elsewhere.

"Do you know any digging songs?" she said.

He shook his head.

"I know a working song," she said, "but not a digging song."

He nodded, plunged his shovel into the dirt and pressed it with his foot. Things were coming up more easily now. The air was cooling off too, which made it only slightly more pleasant to work.

She sang her working song and a few minutes passed more easily. The song was about farming, but there was a little bit in there about the earth and working the dirt and the sun bearing down on you.

Later in the afternoon, the clouds moved in from over the mountains. A light snow began to fall, but it melted as it pressed into the ground. They would dig and dig, then take a break. Bird fetched water from the well and wine from the kitchen, at Mary's request. He set the bottle in the water in its bucket, and carried a loaf of bread in his armpit. The snow kept falling. A thin blanket covered the bodies of the townspeople. Bird felt better already, to see them covered so peacefully. He recommitted to their plan, which was beginning to feel less and less possible.

He gave Mary the wine and bread and re-wrapped the shirt around the palm of his hand. Mary sat down to enjoy all he'd gathered and he set back to work.

"We are doing the right thing," he said.

"Do you think they will come back to haunt us?" said Mary.

"Maybe if we had left them in their houses like they were," said Bird.

"Maybe," she said.

"Do you believe in ghosts?" she said.

"Yes," said Bird.

"Why?"

"Because it is better to believe in them and never see one than not to believe in them when one decides to set upon you."

"You are forever concerned with protection," said Mary. She began to laugh. She was brutally exhausted and giggling.

"It's my hope to be prepared for whatever it is that comes at me next."

"Do you think your arm will come to you as a ghost?" said Mary. "Do you think one morning you will wake and find it there, settled into place as it once was, only blue or white and sort of drifting between this world and the next?" She laughed again. She drank and ate.

"I do not think that," said Bird. He plunged the shovel and leveraged it against his leg again. His strength was not fully in the gesture though, and the dirt rose up but fell back into the hole, rather than to its side. "You could help. You could add depth to the hole as I draw out its side."

"It is important to break and restore your strength. You are going at this like a mad man with only a day to get it done."

164

"I'd like to get it done."

"We have time."

"You'd like to sleep with those people in the street like that?"

"It's snowing," she said.

"Only slightly," he said.

"Still, they will be covered."

"But what about the ghosts," he said.

"There is no such thing," she said.

Bird removed a knife from his belt and considered it.

"Do you have a knife?" he said.

She did not.

"But you can get one?"

She could.

"We'll take their teeth," he said.

"I don't know what you mean."

"We'll bury their teeth. Bury their ghosts."

"That is horrid and I've never heard of such a thing."

"Will you help or not?"

"I will not," she said.

As the sun began to set and the evening grew cool, they retreated to their building with the kitchen. The bodies lined up in the street were nothing more than row after row of raised snow, like a plowed field in winter. The blood was only faintly visible beneath the thinner layers, and it was vanishing with each passing moment.

Neither of them was in any condition to cook a meal, so they ate what was left of the bread with salt and stoked the fire and huddled together. Bird's hand was well-worn and bloody. Mary's hands were blistered and ready to pop. She rinsed the wounds with cool water, and bandaged each. It snowed steadily on outside. For the first time since they'd left home, they slept soundly through the night.

They woke to find the village covered in several feet of snow, with more of it still in the air. The rows Bird had set out were unidentifiable. The hole, on which they had worked so tirelessly, was filled now with snow and marked only by the snow-capped mound of dirt at its side.

The snow stayed with them for days. They dug out the store of logs lining the back of the building with the kitchen, and stacked them inside to thaw and dry. Most would not burn at first, but those that did warmed and worked to dry the others. They made more bread. Bird practiced with the pistol, although Mary insisted he do so upstairs. The sound of it startled her, but no matter of fussing or demanding would stop him.

He was closing off to her. He seemed distracted and uncomfortable. He would end what might have become a perfectly good conversation by refusing to answer with more than a single word.

"Do you think we might develop some land, when the snow stops?"

"No."

"Would you like a family some day? Do you believe this town could restore itself? If we help, maybe? Do you think we could keep this town in some kind of decent shape, for when more people come? When the town grows again?"

To this, he said nothing. He was watching out the window. The snow was burying them. It wouldn't stay forever. They could dig themselves out and get back to work. They had only a few more days of this. A week at most. They were not trapped. They were not in danger. They had only to wait.

† † †

The infant would not stop screaming. She had no milk for it, no liquid with which to feed it. Only a few scraps of food and the snow she could melt in her hands for drinking. She chewed a bit of dried beef and tried to spit it into the baby's mouth, but it would not accept it. She rode on through the night and put the sun at her back as it began to rise. The horse was flagging. She was flagging. The baby was screaming and screaming and screaming. She did not know this baby. She did not have the body warmth to keep it alive. She did not know the man she had killed. From what she could tell, everyone from the town was dead. Everyone except for Mary and Bird. And they needed her. She had to survive for them and find her way back. She rode until the horse began to falter. She pushed it a bit farther and it finally bent its front knees and brought her down into the snow. The baby fell from her. It disappeared into several feet of snow without a sound, like a twig into a canyon. But then it began to scream again. The horse's hocks gave then and she was suddenly in the snow and thanking the heavens that the horse had not crushed her. The child would not stop screaming. She had made a poor decision, coming out here. She had put herself at risk and the child was no better off. She had pursued the man unthinkingly and brought herself to this low point. There was no way of anticipating the snowfall. Now the snow would fall and it would keep falling and falling, as the baby kept screaming and screaming.

It was difficult to move. She wasn't pinned, but was bound up by her clothing and finding it hard to lift or turn. She dropped to her side, into the snow and shook her sleeves back from her wrists, opening up the space around her elbows. Snow poured in, wedged itself between her coat and dress, and began to melt.

She lifted herself onto an elbow and rose. She separated herself from the horse. It turned onto its side, obviously disliking the snow but without the strength to rise and shake it from its hair. She shook what she could from her arms and torso and lifted the baby from its pocket of snow. She removed a crude knife from the few belongings she'd taken from the man she'd killed. She plunged the knife into the belly of the horse and brought it down. The horse screamed and thrashed and landed a blow to her side, likely cracking a rib. She rose and opened the animal, releasing a pocket of steam. Blood and slick innards she could not identify spilled onto the snow for a moment but then seemed to reach an equilibrium and come to rest. The horse protested then, but only for a moment before going still. She wrapped herself around the infant and squeezed whatever parts of herself she could into the horse's husk. Everything from her waist up was still exposed. Her legs were slick and sliding out. Nothing would stay put. She warmed slightly, but not for long. Her pants were wet now. There was nothing to set her heels upon. Nothing that would hold her. Only the snow and the meat and the hard bits she slid from. The baby was still screaming. She couldn't think, so she didn't try to.

Brooke started thinking about love once the snow began to fall. He'd met his wife during a brutal snowstorm, many years ago. The circumstances weren't far from those of his current situation. He'd left the riders he was with. He'd struck out on his own. They were getting a reputation, and with that came a sense of obligation to this or that, and they started spending more time deciding who they were going to hunt down and how than actually getting after it. It wasn't a bitter parting, but a necessary one. Hunting or no, they took the desert paths when they could. Slept in caves or alongside springs. It was by riding with these men that he had learned how to best survive the situation in which he'd currently found himself. He knew it well. Even if life did not repeat itself, there were certainly echoes that rang out forever. He had no doubt that he could survive out here for as long as it would take him to find the next place to be. There was water. Some plants. He didn't need much. It wasn't fun, and he was losing weight like a broken bucket drains water, but he could keep it all going if he had to.

It was clean. Or clean enough, their parting. They'd stopped for water and Brooke told one of the men he was thinking of riding off and trying to see if the rumors were true about making money digging in the earth. There were stories all the time about men finding a life's fortune in rocks or oil, just under the sand, or in their own backyards. He figured he would take a stab at it. Ride out a bit and see what he could find.

"So you're done here?" said the man.

Brooke could not picture his face.

"I think so," he said, or something equally plain.

And that was that. The man Brooke could not remember went to the water to fill his canteen like every other man, and Brooke rode on. He had no interest at all in digging in the dirt, but it was time to get away. Going off on your own was enough like greed to be made sense of and not resented. These men understood greed. They even liked it, provided it did not interfere with a plan. Some of the most pleasurable exchanges they had over the campfire were about all the rotten things they'd done, or all that had gone wrong, in pursuit of a dollar or two, or a woman, or both.

Brooke had been full of stories then, full of the lives of all those men. He'd felt as if he'd lived one hundred lives. Walking up and down along this desert creek now, it was hard to distinguish this from that, or to remember who said what or how any story ended or began. There was a lot of middle. A lot of in between. The edges of each tale were worn and indistinguishable.

He remembered that one man was able to escape a hanging because the sheriff who had captured him left the cell unlocked. How such a thing could have happened, or what the man had done after, Brooke had no sense of. He remembered picturing the man's hand as it came down upon the cell door to rest, and the door just squeaking open then, and all the joy and surprise the man must have felt realizing that he had back his freedom.

Many of the men at his side had lost their families. Most to violence, a few to disease. Some to their own bad habits of drinking or gambling. Brooke's head was filled with images of outfits, gangs, marauders, riding right up to a ranch's front door and taking everything they pleased then destroying the rest. That was just the way of things. They themselves weren't so different. Between each of the towns was pure wilderness, and what came bearing down upon civilization was beyond imagination, for most. He'd seen plenty, but he was still capable of surprise. He was not hardened to a measure of awe and respect for what the wilderness was capable of producing. Snow was bearing down upon him. Snow was obscuring the rocks and shrubs and horizon. The stream was still undeniably at his side, but if the snow kept up it would freeze and get buried with the rest. Brooke was now of the mind that once a thing began there was no use in expecting it to end any place short of total devastation. The first few flakes of snow signaled an impending snowstorm, regardless of how the sky looked. He was to be severed from and discarded by the world. Here and now, he would meet his quiet end.

Or so he'd expected. And then she'd appeared, on the horizon, moving slowly toward him. He hadn't even realized that he was collapsed until she was at his side and encouraging him to sit up, to drink and open his eyes. She was weeping as if it moved her to see him like this. As if she'd known him. She had something sick within her. Her eyes were not warm, but nearly white, like those of a fish. She twisted water from the ends of her sleeves and the tail of her shirt and washed his face and the inside of his mouth. Her touch was not loving, not yet, but was confident and familiar, as if she'd made a life of rescuing half-dead men from the wilderness.

"Are you lost?" she said.

She held him in her lap. The snow fell steadily.

He nodded.

"I am lost too," she said.

He nodded. When he woke, she had his back propped against her front. His legs were in the snow, sunk to the bottom and greeting the sand down below them. She had spread out a blanket beneath her. It dipped toward the center where she sat, and was slowly filling with snow. You could not see the sky. Only the sun and the thick, broken snow, as if it were falling directly from heaven. The wind picked up and moved the snow around and then it seemed to be coming directly from the earth, spiraling up and around and holding them there.

"You fell asleep," she said.

He nodded.

It was more than likely that he had died. That this woman was an angel or some creature made entirely of death. He could hardly feel how cold it looked. He could not make sense of where he'd been and where he was now.

"It wasn't snowing only a few days before," he said.

"It was not snowing when I set out," she said.

"What were you after?" he said.

"A baby," she said.

"Whose baby?" he said.

"I do not know," she said.

He did not press her anymore. He wanted her to continue, but was not sure when her sickness would expose itself. There was something wrong in her, and he did not want to face it. He had no defenses and was enjoying her warmth and company.

"Are you married?" he said.

"I was," she said.

She leaned into him, to warm or to quiet him. Her hair smelled rotten, like death and sweat. Her fingernails were stained through with crud. She had dirt in the cracks of her knuckles. Scratches on her face and neck. Something about her was incredibly beautiful to him.

"You've been through hell," he said, and she did not respond.

When the windows were fully covered, there was no clear way to determine the weather. They knew it was cold, so they knew that the snow had not melted and was not melting. They knew they were running low on logs and chairs and tables for the fire. They were not running low on food, and water could be made from the snow easily enough. They had a small pouch of bullets that Bird had acquired from the homes he'd broken into when retrieving the bodies. So he did not fire the gun when he practiced his aim. He merely practiced keeping the pistol steady.

His single arm extended, he would shut an eye and attach the barrel of his gun to some small item on the room's far wall. He would hold steady, count to see how long he held, and begin again every time the barrel shifted or his breath drew him out of alignment. Mary did not much like the game, and told him so repeatedly. But he did not stop.

He explored the second floor and found magazines and adventure books in a trunk beneath one of the beds. He brought them down with the thread from before. He taught himself to thread a needle with a single hand, using his knees and wetting the string with his mouth to keep it stable and pointed. He believed this would help him with his aim, in the long run. He asked Mary to read the magazines and adventure books aloud to him.

"Men are not like that," said Bird.

"You do not know all the men in the world," said Mary.

"Women are not like that," said Bird.

"With that," said Mary, "I can agree."

Bird began to work on his speed. He tucked the pistol into a pocket and withdrew it as quickly as possible. Often, it fell. Once, it went off. Snow came in through the fresh hole in the window. Mary took the gun and unloaded it. She demanded the bullets from his pouch. They were getting along as well as they ever had.

Mary did not like the books at first. She said they lacked the right kind of description, and they did not conclude in a high-minded way. But while Bird was practicing with his pistol, she had little else to do other than read and reread them. She was not interested in pistols. She was not willing to cook any more than he was, and so they prepared nothing more than they had to. She did not like to explore upstairs. She tinkered at the piano, but produced no sounds that pleased her. It needed tuning. She had never been a pianist, and now it made her think too much of Martha, and of how long they had been there, and of how long they could be stuck. But they were not stuck, it was important to remember. They could tunnel out. They would tunnel out. Or the snow would melt. *We will not die like this*, she told herself.

"Do you think, when Martha returns, she'll be able to find us?"

"She's not coming back," said Bird.

"But do you think we're buried so far now that it looks only like a desert of snow? Can you even see the town as you approach?"

"How much snow could there be?"

"We are covered," she said, "and who knows how high it goes?"

"It cannot go on forever," said Bird. "It has to stop somewhere."

He withdrew his pistol and held it steady. He placed it back behind his belt.

"Do you think the bodies will be as we left them?"

"No," he said.

"You've grown cold," she said.

"There is snow everywhere," he said.

"Do you love me like a husband loves a wife?" she said.

"I don't know," he said.

"I feel like we are supposed to become husband and wife," she said.

"Why?"

"Because we are here together and alone together and we get along and there is no one else."

"There will be others someday," he said.

"Do you really think so?" she said.

"Yes," he said.

"I will be happy to see them," she said.

"I won't," he said. "But I'll be ready."

It went on like this for longer than either of them realized. It was always dark, always cold. The fire gave them just enough heat and light to get by, but they didn't allow themselves much more than that. There was no knowing how long they would have to keep it going.

They had no way of knowing for sure which day the snow stopped. But suddenly water was running in through the hole in the window, and seeping in through the cracks in the wood and where the building's joints were not flush or tight. It kept on like this and they soon realized that the snow was melting without pause. Which meant the sun was out. Which meant the days and nights were warming. Suddenly, the whole room would creak when Bird traveled up the stairs, so Mary made him promise to stop.

"All this snow came and held us here," she said, "and now it's going."

She was smiling.

He nodded.

They slept on the two remaining tables to keep out of the damp. The floor was soggy. Their clothes would not dry. Their time in the building with the kitchen was nearly up.

Bird was the first to dig out, but only slightly. The snow outside was mere slush piled high, and little canals ran the water out into the wilderness around them. In every direction you could hear the sound of water running. He imagined himself a gunslinger, running the water out of town. He was able to get the door open, but not without letting in a considerable amount of slush. He was able then to dig a few inches out onto the porch. The snow level was near the roof now, but crumbling. Disappearing. Hightailing it. He took to the stairs though he had promised not to do so. He looked out the windows and could see the tops of trees again. He could see the tall rocks in the distance. He could smell the air the sun had touched. He could feel the sun as it broke through the glass. He followed its beam around the room. He wanted to get a sunburn. That was his goal. A sunburn on his single exposed arm. Or on his face and neck. He could feel it cooking him. He heard a fly buzzing at the window and almost burst into tears.

"We are nearly out," said Mary.

"Nearly," said Bird.

"What will we do?"

"We'll leave," he said.

"Where will we go?"

"We."

"I will go where you go," said Mary.

"I'm going to follow the trail that brought us here."

"That will lead us home," she said.

"I will keep following it, on past the ranch where I was nursed, and I will hunt down the men who put me there."

"John killed that thing," said Mary.

"Not that thing," said Bird.

"Then what?"

"The men who killed my family," said Bird.

"Are you out of your wits? You're acting stranger than I've yet seen you act."

"I'm clear-headed," said Bird, "and I've a simple plan that will guide me through the next period of my life."

"A murderous plan?"

He nodded.

"I do not approve."

"You don't have to."

"As long as you know."

"I've always known," said Bird. "You do not have to speak on it."

"Known what?"

"That you don't approve."

"Of what?"

"Of me. Of my plans. Of the way I think of things."

"How do you think of them?"

"You know clearly well how I think of them and what I expect of the world."

"Horridness and dread."

He did not respond.

"You expect only the worst."

He did not respond.

"You do."

"No. But I am prepared for the worst thing. I will work against the worst thing with everything I have within me."

"Murderously."

"Yes."

"But murder is that worst thing you are preparing for."

"No, it isn't."

"It is up there on the list of worst things then."

"Depending on the circumstances, yes. John's murder was a worst thing. The men who killed my family was a worst thing. The man who took Martha was a worst thing."

"Do you know who killed your family?"

"Two men killed my family and brought me into the woods

with them when I was much smaller than I am now. They tried to raise me or hold me hostage, but then they turned on me. I cannot remember everything. I will never be in that position again. I will fight that position with everything that's within me."

It was a line he'd drawn from one of the adventure books. There was a man who wore the same hat daily and fought evil with everything that was within him.

"You will die," she said.

He nodded.

"And you are likely to do an accidental wrong."

"Not if I pay attention," he said. "And not if the world watches out for me."

"These men," said Mary. "What color were their hats?"

"They did not wear hats," said Bird.

"What were their faces like? Did they have any scars?"

Bird shook his head. "I do not know."

"How will you know them then?" she said.

"I will know the feeling of being near them."

"I will not read you any more from those books," she said.

"You have read enough."

The next day, the sun broke finally from beneath the rooftop. It lit the edges of the room in which they slept. They woke to it. They wept. Time itself had freed them. They ate the jerky they had been saving. It was salty and tough, but a treat nonetheless. It stung the roofs of their mouths and puckered the edges of their lips. The sun. There it was. Mary sang a song about the sun. Bird practiced with his pistol.

Everything, then, seemed connected to her. When the snow stopped, it was because she had brought hope to the world. When the sun came out, it was to echo her filthy beauty. Brooke fed her from the desert and the stream and she held him. They did not walk together, but sat and let the snow vanish and the creek widen. The air was suddenly warm enough for exposed sleep. The stars were out. The sky was thick with them. Throughout the day, the moon was as clear as a treetop in the distance. She did not seem to sleep. She cried every so often. He slept on her, where she would let him. His head on a thigh, or a leg thrown over hers, if she was also sleeping. When she began to warble late in the night, he simply rolled away. She did not speak much. He told her what he'd found for them to eat, or how he'd caught it. Told her how to eat the spiny things, or the smallest creatures with the most delicate flavor. He was perfectly content to sit with her, day after day, in the mud and vanishing snow. It still sat atop the red rocks towering in the distance.

"Which way did you come from?" he asked. "Are we near a town?"

She shook her head.

"I was lost in the storm for some time before I found you," she said.

That was heartwarming to him. The idea that, with him, she did not consider herself lost. He left it at that. He was eating no more than before, a little less, in fact, but he felt he was getting some of his old strength back. He felt he could last a little longer. That he wanted to last a little longer. He was curious what was in store for them. He imagined she would stay with him forever, seeing as it felt so right as it was.

She avoided locking eyes with the horizon. She kept her gaze on nearby things: her hands, the food he was providing, the water, the soles of her feet, the edges of the blanket. She was in no hurry to get anywhere, and that was more than fine to Brooke.

One night, he set a hand on the delicate tissue between her legs. She was on her back, her legs apart. He set his palm there, on the outside of her leggings. She did not react. He rotated his hand in a small circle, as he had done with Sugar, years before. She did not react. He kept it up, brought himself onto an elbow and leaned toward her. She was fixated on the clots of stars above them.

In the morning, he woke and she was gone. He was on the muddy blanket, alone and sweating in the sun. He heard voices, horses, active wood. He turned and discovered the wagon train, its carts and carriers still in a tight line, its travelers scattered across the landscape. Some were resting in the shadows of the wagons. Some were collecting water from the stream, passing around a cupped pan. There were four men and two women. The eldest of the group was of indeterminate age, a weathered old man sporting a beard and perched on a rock. They had a few mules and several horses, both harnessed and un-harnessed. He could not spot her. He gathered himself up and brought himself over to the older man sitting on a small rock beside several young men. Brooke tried to speak, but his voice was tired and unpracticed.

"I've been lost," he said.

"We know," said the older man. He put out his hand. "I'm the Pa here."

"Hello, Pa."

"My name is Wendell."

"Hello, Wendell."

"These are my boys: Jack, Marston, and Clay."

Each of them had the man's face at some previous stage. It

was like standing before a row of daguerreotypes taken at ten- or twenty-year intervals. The youngest seemed about eighteen or so.

"Howdy," said Brooke.

"Your wife's in the wagon. She's ill and needs to be cared for," said Wendell.

"Which wagon?" said Brooke.

"That," said Wendell.

Brooke shook the boys' hands and nodded to Wendell and walked toward the far wagon containing the woman he'd met in the snow. He lifted himself on the wagon's step and peered into the back.

An older woman and a child were at the woman's side. The child was holding her hand and the older woman was mixing something in a small bowl.

"What's she sick with?" asked Brooke.

"You must be John," said the girl holding her hand.

Brooke nodded.

"Some kind of fever," she said.

"She'll be all right?" said Brooke.

They both nodded. The woman with the small bowl applied its contents to the sick woman's lips. It was a red paste of some kind. From where Brooke stood, it had no smell.

"She's just out of sorts," said the woman applying the paste. "She needs to rest and eat. You can ride with us as far as you like. From what she's told us, you can handle providing sustenance for the two of you."

Brooke nodded. "As long as we stay by the stream. And as long as it doesn't start snowing again."

"Wasn't that something?" said the girl holding her hand. She was younger, by fifty years or so. A granddaughter, maybe.

181

"It was not easy going," said the woman applying the paste. "I imagine it was particularly difficult for the two of you, out here alone as you were."

Brooke nodded.

"She says you've been wandering for some time?"

Brooke nodded.

"My guess is that you're not opposed to joining up with us?"

"We could use your medical help. A few days off of our feet," said Brooke.

"Most of us walk," said the woman applying the paste. "Alongside or behind the wagons. The more the horses have to carry, the more often we have to stop, and the greater the risk of exhausting them or losing them to injury. She'll have to rest here for a while, but you'll have to do your part."

Brooke nodded.

"I can manage that," he said.

"It is a nice surprise to meet new people," said the girl holding her hand. "We've been walking for so long, and my brothers really aren't much for company."

Brooke nodded.

"Do you and your wife have a family looking for you?" said the older woman. She set down the bowl and began to blow on the sick woman's pasted lips.

"I have a brother," he said. "But I have not seen him for some time. I do not know what's become of him."

"I'm sorry to hear that," said the girl holding her hand.

Brooke nodded.

A shout from Wendell set the horses to a steady pace, and the other travelers fell in line alongside the wagon train. Brooke lowered himself from the wagon as it startled into motion, and told the women he would be back later to check on his wife.

182

Then they walked. The man introduced as Marston led three ponies at the rear of the wagon train. He was not skilled at moving them. They gave him great grief, and he tugged their reins and poked at their muzzles with a thin switch. Brooke took pace to the right of the third wagon, nearest the back. None in the party seemed concerned with him. None spoke to one another, or sang any songs.

When they stopped, for water or for rest, he checked on his wife. She was on the edge of sleep for nearly two days, never fully in or out. She spoke to him, but he could not make sense of it. She told him that the earth had begged her for the child. That the earth had told her it wasn't hers and she could not care for it. She had wanted to help the child, she assured him. She had set out to perform good. She was losing her mind as his was slowly coming back to him. His memories faded, his reflections on all he had done before and how it had led him here. He was more and more simply there. He watched the female members of the wagon train. He had many ideas about them, but kept them all to himself. One was either slow-witted, or had a damaged speech capacity. She spoke at a slant, from the corner of her mouth. She did not say much, but when she did, it was about the wind, or about her clothing. She chased down a rag as it was drawn several hundred feet from the caravan by the wind. She clutched it to her body. So far off, she looked like a scraggly tree. Wendell fired a shot into the air, which startled her and brought her running back toward them. Another woman, her sister or cousin, wore muddy clothes and often spoke with Wendell privately, in hushed tones. It was Brooke's assumption that these two had conspired to mobilize the family. They seemed to carry the weight of the trip. They made the decisions for when to stop and when to go, when to set up camp. Brooke's best guess was that the woman was Wendell's daughter. She seemed roughly twenty-five years his younger, and there was nothing in their body language to suggest they were intimate.

The woman caring for Brooke's wife introduced herself as Wendell's sister. They'd made camp after several hours of slowly working their way back in the direction from which Brooke had first started out. They were headed back to the corpses of the men who had captured him, the stagecoach that had once been his transport.

Marston pulled a crate of rocks from the back of one wagon and arranged them into a circle for the fire pit. He dug a shallow hole, spitting and cursing as he did. He was thin and not well suited to the work.

"My name is Irene," said Wendell's sister. She offered Brooke a sip of water from a thin aluminum saucer.

Brooke accepted, but took only enough to show he appreciated the offering.

"John," said Brooke.

"Right," said Irene. "How long have you and your wife been on foot?"

Brooke shrugged. "The only honest answer is that I lost count."

"Where are you headed?"

"My wife and I," said Brooke, "we lost a child not too long ago."

"I know," said Irene. "She's said as much."

"She has been wandering ever since, and I have been following her. At first, I tried to stop her, but she would not be stopped."

Irene nodded.

"Dorothy lost hers," she said. She gestured to the woman

who spoke at a slant. "Some six years ago, maybe? It was born dead."

Brooke nodded.

"She is lucky to have survived," said Brooke. "I've seen a stillborn do much more damage."

"We are lucky," said Irene. "I'm not sure what she is."

"We won't be any trouble to you all," said Brooke.

"I know," said Irene.

"We appreciate your help. We'll uncouple ourselves from you at the first town we come to, if you like. I think my wife needs a bed and a good meal. Maybe we'll find a small place to call our own. We had a ranch once, but we cannot go back there."

Irene nodded.

"Haints stay where and as they please," she said.

Because of the snow, the creek was enormous now and moving quickly. There was less food to be found, but there was still food to be found. When they slept, they tied the horses together and blocked the wagon's wheels. Many of them chose to sleep outside, beneath the stars. Wendell and his sister took to one of the wagons. Brooke slept in the third wagon, beside the woman he met in the snow. She spoke throughout the night, every so often. Some bit of nonsense or another. She took no notice of him. He listened to her for some time before he began to respond.

"I was told to do as I did," she said.

"By the earth," he said.

"I could feel I'd done wrong as soon as I did it."

"I know that feeling," said Brooke. "I have felt it often."

"It would not stop screaming," she said.

"It goes away," said Brooke.

"Until I put it down, it would not stop."

"But then it stopped," said Brooke.

She began to cry then.

"Then it stopped," she said.

The bodies were waterlogged and delicate. Bird lifted the arm of a young man and the skin shifted, the body cracked as if Bird could tear loose the limb without much more than a tug. He dropped the arm and retreated to Mary where she stood on the porch, her hands over her eyes, still speaking out in protest.

"You must stop," she said.

"We cannot move them," he said.

"You should not," she said.

"It would be impossible," said Bird. "They are too full of water and too far gone. We cannot move them."

"We have to leave," said Mary.

Finally, Bird agreed.

Mary spent the evening preparing food for the journey: baking loaves of bread and gathering butter, salt, and cured meat into manageable sacks to be carried on their backs. Bird checked the houses again and found more bullets, another pistol, rotten meal, and some more jerky. The houses groaned as he moved through them. They were each tilted on their foundation, sagging and heavy with water. The roofs of several had already collapsed. He moved through them, navigating the rubble. They were lit cleanly by the blue sky above. He found two more bodies. Two children huddled in a basement. He covered them with blankets from a nearby dresser. He did not mention them to Mary.

They set out for the woods. Mary walked in front and Bird took up the rear. He carried several sacks on his shoulder, but dropped them again and again, claiming to have heard some sound or another. Birds launched from bushes and startled him into withdrawing his pistol. And every time, in order to do so, he had to drop the sacks.

"You'll mush the bread," said Mary. "You mustn't drop them."

"Carry a pistol then," said Bird.

She took one, but did not like it and kept it unloaded.

"It is no good that way," said Bird.

"I will not shoot off my foot," said Mary, "carrying a loaded pistol in my belt and with several sacks in each arm. I'll do things my way."

They had to stop often. The sacks were too much for them. They kept the sun behind them. Mary insisted there were several towns founded at the far edge of the forest, directly opposite the desert towns. She had never traveled from one to the other, but John had, and had told her as much. At the far end of the woods would be either mountains or a town where they could eat proper food and find some safety. They walked for hours and hours, until the sun began to set. Mary did not like it one bit. Each step was painful and unpleasant and the bags kept slipping and swinging and making her gait unsteady. Bird was silent. He seemed neither comfortable nor struggling. She made the decision not to complain, though there was plenty to complain about.

"We've probably walked fifteen miles," said Mary. "Maybe even twenty."

"I don't think so," said Bird.

"How many do you think?"

"Five," he said. "Or six. Hardly any. These bags are slowing everything down, and you keep stopping. So we're crawling."

On the far side of the woods, she would consider the

possibility of leaving his side. She had thought about it long and hard and she did not want to marry him. She wanted to marry someone nicer and smarter. Bird was a violent nuisance. There was nothing to him that made her want to stay.

Bird insisted that they cover themselves when they slept. What the blankets could not reach, a sack would cover. The more they seemed to be a pile, the better. He slept with a bag of bread on his face. Mary found it funny and refused to do so. The treetops seemed miles above them. They tilted and groaned in the wind. She wanted to consider them as she prepared herself for sleep.

"If you are spotted," said Bird, "we will have trouble."

"I have a pistol," she said.

"You will get us both tortured, eaten, or killed," said Bird.

"That is silly," she said.

She knew it wasn't silly. She was carrying twice the sacks he was able to because the woods had shown him precisely what there was to be afraid of. Still, she had her pistol, and was intelligent and strong, and she would not be told over and over again by him what to do and how to feel. They were not a family and they were not in love. The moon was out, and it was full.

The next day went much as the previous. They walked and stopped and walked and stopped. They found a small stream and drank from it. They filled their canteens and a cup to carry each. Mary spotted a bird's nest with a mother bird on its edge. She did not mention it to Bird.

"I like it out here," said Mary. "It is pretty and I like the air."

"You're a fool to fall in love with it," said Bird.

She did not answer. The mother bird lifted and sought food for the hidden young.

"You would do better to speak less," said Mary.

"The same could be said of you," said Bird.

"Perhaps," she said. "But you are predictable and your position is clear. If you said nothing, I would nonetheless know how you felt about anything we might experience."

"How do I feel about what you've just said?"

"You feel hurt, perhaps, but you also think that I am wrong."

"I am not hurt."

That night, Bird was less insistent about the sacks. He did not cover his face, and said nothing when Mary set her blanket down on the ground, rather than over her bright muddy white dress.

They were quiet for some time, but neither slept.

"Do you know any constellations?" said Mary.

"What are they?"

"The stars," said Mary. "The shapes they make."

"I see clusters," said Bird, "flickering like a bunch of little fires on the hill."

"Several points make an identifiable shape," said Mary. "If you imagine a line drawn between them."

"Like what?"

"I have only been told of them, and I do not know them," said Mary. "So every time I look, they are different."

"What are they now?"

"I am too tired to see anything other than a big soft bed for me to sleep in."

"I will make money in town and we will buy a big soft bed," said Bird.

Mary did not respond.

It was a cold night. The trees seemed not to break the wind at all. The mouths of the bread sacks slapped the earth and neither of their blankets would hold still. They hardly slept. They lay awake, staring up and trying to settle things. In the morning, they walked. They walked and walked and walked. They were losing their appetites, though they were working harder than they had for some time. When they were alone in the building with the kitchen, the amount of bread it took to fill them up was less and less with each day. Typically, they were still hungry after they were finished eating, but their stomachs could take no more of what it was they had to give it. In the woods, even that small amount seemed too much to the both of them. They forced it down, knowing they needed the energy to keep themselves on foot and moving forward. It was painful and Mary would throw up every now and then, after a meal. When she did, Bird made them stop and eat more. She knew he was right, that she needed to eat, but it was miserable and she hated him for it.

On the fourth day, the trees broke and they discovered a meadow. There were white flowers scattered throughout, and clusters of yellow ones. Bees crowded the blossoms. At the far end of the meadow, a thick brown moose vanished back into the woods.

On the fifth day, Bird spotted a fence. They had crossed the meadow and back into the trees. These trees were thinner, more spread apart. Finally, they gave way to a slope of rolling hills. It was on the edge of one of these hills that Bird saw the shadow of four parallel lines, breaking the light that was vanishing beyond it.

"On the other side of that hill," said Bird, "we will find a house."

Mary did not believe it. Or she was not willing to let herself believe it. That this early on, they would discover a home, a fireplace, a matching set of chairs and people in them.

They walked on and discovered it was true. They spotted the

smoke first, and then the ponies. Trained ponies moving about within the confines of the enormous gate. They investigated the two of them from a comfortable distance. The pen was large enough to vanish over a second hill, and it was the hill from behind which the smoke was rising. It was blue in the dusk light, lifting casually and thinning.

"I would like to pet them," said Mary.

"Do as you like," said Bird. He set down his sacks. He removed his pistol from his belt and approached the far hill. He crested it, kept low, and descended toward the house. He spotted no bodies on the porch or in the distance of any visible direction. It was a log cabin, relatively new. He crept to the window and crouched there. He listened, but heard nothing. Then he heard the floorboards groan. He spotted a cat lapping water from a puddle by the porch. A young girl appeared at its edge. She set herself on her belly, reached down and gripped the cat, and it scratched her. She began to cry, and an older man appeared behind her to investigate.

"Who are you?" said the man.

He held his daughter behind him then.

"What do you want?"

Bird had the pistol trained on him. He was trembling.

"Are you hurt?" said the man.

Bird did not respond.

The cat bounded beneath the porch. The girl's head appeared to the right of her father's hip.

"He's lost an arm," she said.

"Are you hurt?" the man said again.

"No," said Bird. "Where is the nearest town?"

"About ten miles up that road," said the man, pointing to a

path leading from the front of the house. "Are you here to hurt or rob us?"

"No," said Bird. "But we'd like to eat."

"We?"

"My wife and I," said Bird.

"But you can't be more than... fourteen?" said the man.

"I am older than that," said Bird. "We've been walking for days."

"From where?"

"The woods," said Bird, "that way." He signaled with the barrel of the pistol then directed it back at the man.

"Wolf Creek? But it's winter..."

Bird did not respond.

"You were in the valley when it snowed?"

Bird nodded.

"With your parents?"

Bird did not respond.

"Alone then."

"I want to meet his wife," said the man's daughter. She was all the way out at his side now, gripping his hand as he held it to her.

"She's with the ponies," said Bird.

"I don't want her fooling with those ponies," said the man. "I aim to sell them."

"She just wanted to meet them," said Bird.

"I don't want her fooling with them. If you go get her, and put that pistol away, we'll give you some supper and I can hitch you into town in the morning."

"Where will we sleep?"

"We've got furs and a floor," said the man.

"I'd just as soon sleep out here," said Bird.

"In the mud?"

Bird nodded.

"Fine by me," said the man. "Now go get your wife and tell her not to fool with those ponies."

Brooke made himself useful. He answered to Wendell, but more than that, he aided Marston and Clay when he was done with any particular assigned task. He dug the fire pits—they often had two or three going a night. He dug latrines and led the more troublesome horses. He offered rest to the weary. He offered bits of the food he caught, a bite of rabbit to the youngest girl after he and his wife were fed. He fell in line with their party, and they absorbed him. His wife was slowly recovering. Some mornings, she rose and walked with him. Other days, she spent alone in the shade and relative comfort of the wagon.

Soon, they came upon the large rocks Brooke had not forgotten. Jack spotted the wreckage, and he, Marston, and Clay rode out to investigate it. The others rested. The boys reported that it was a hired stagecoach, containing several corpses. There had likely been a robbery. There were no tracks, and the corpses were far gone. Whoever had taken down the stagecoach had emptied it of whatever contents were of value and were now gone from the area. It was likely that the wagon train was safe from harm, and that they should continue as they had been.

"Did you investigate the rocks?" said Wendell. "Did you check for caves?"

"We found two caves," said Marston. "They were empty. There was yellow water in one and we filled the reserve canteens."

"You shouldn't drink yellow water," said Wendell.

"We've marked them for emergencies only," said Marston.

They set on again.

That night, Brooke boiled the yellow water and strained it through several layers of fabric and sand. It cleared slightly. The smell lifted. He drank a small amount in front of Wendell to show that it was trustworthy. The party waited one day, kept an eye on Brooke, who showed no signs of suffering or discontent. By the end of the day, they were sipping from the reserve canteens. Wendell sent Marston back to the cave to fill anything that could be capped. There was no telling when they would encounter water again. They had left the creek some days before, and now the only water was that which gathered in muddy puddles along their path, and sprang from the occasional hoof print. Brooke volunteered to ride with Marston.

They took the two fastest horses. It was not far at all to backtrack without the wagons and the slow pace of their train. As they reached the stagecoach, Marston did not pause, but Brooke slowed his ride.

"What do you think they were transporting?" said Brooke.

"Gold," said Marston. "Or someone influential. Perhaps a gang leader or a prisoner or a political figure. The men were armed. They wore holsters and pouches. Whatever it was is gone, though. The cave's to the left. In that larger of the two red rocks." He gestured with the reins of his horse in the direction he was headed.

Brooke dismounted and examined the stagecoach. It was nearly unrecognizable with all the weather had done.

"Must have been gold," Brooke yelled to Marston. "The back seat is a hollowed bench, emptied."

Marston was just beyond earshot. He signaled for Brooke to join him, so Brooke mounted his horse and rode to meet the man.

"The back seat is a hollow bench," said Brooke.

"So it was gold," said Marston.

"Looks like," said Brooke.

"Imagine," said Marston, "even if it were still all there to be collected, Wendell would not allow us to take it."

"Why's that?"

"Too heavy. An unnecessary burden. We would be sore to leave it but he would figure it the same as if we had never found it."

"And you all listen to him?"

"Always have," said Marston.

"And he brought you out here?"

"It was a group decision. It is this one," said Marston. They entered the cave, filled all they had to fill, and climbed back upon their horses.

"But it was his idea?" said Brooke.

"Wendell has fond memories of Wolf Creek," said Marston. They rode at a good clip for some time then, slowed when they spotted the wagon train in the distance.

"And what did you think?" said Brooke.

"That it would not be as he remembered it," said Marston. "But we were out of money and nothing would grow, so we needed a new plan."

"You sold your land and headed out."

Marston nodded. "Bought the wagons and what else we could with the money."

"What is Wolf Creek?"

"A town in a valley. Small, fertile, lonesome. I've only heard stories. Snows come in every so often and wreak all kinds of havoc. The valley'll fill up in the worst of them. Heard a family died one winter, holding out for the snow to pass. Most people use it as a place to stop off in between."

"In between what?"

"Where they're coming from and where they're going," said Marston. "There's water there. And cheap land. We don't have to stay forever."

"How long have you been moving?"

"A long time," said Marston.

They were quiet then. They joined the train shortly after and separated.

The woman Brooke met in the snow was up and walking alongside Irene.

"John has come back," said Irene.

The woman looked at him, confused for a moment, and then smiled.

Brooke lowered himself from his horse and loaded the water into the back of the wagon. That evening, he treated the water and sat with the woman he met in the snow. She watched him and learned the routine, then set to treating some of the water herself.

"It doesn't get rid of everything," said Brooke, "but it tastes a little better and the smell goes away."

"Is it still dangerous?"

"Not really," said Brooke. "It might come out your far end a little aggressively, but you'll recover and it won't happen again. Your stomach gets stronger like an arm." He flexed.

"You are not John," she said.

"I know," said Brooke.

"I do not know you."

"We met by the creek while you were wandering. I was wandering too," said Brooke. "You saved my life." He poured the water slowly and steadily over the handmade filter.

"I remember," she said.

196

"Who was John?" he said.

"My husband," she said.

"Where is John?" he said.

"Gone."

He nodded.

"Why didn't you tell them?"

"I am tired," she said. "They trust us. They like you. You have not asked much of me. We can continue as we are, if it suits you as well."

"It suits me," he said.

"You are not a bad man?" she said.

"No," he said.

"But you have done wrong," she said.

"In the past," he said. "But not with you."

"You see that it remains the case," she said.

The water was treated and safely stored. It was a warm night, so they slept on their backs in the dirt, without a fire.

In the morning, Brooke sought out Marston. He was unblocking the wagon wheels and digging the anchoring stakes from the dirt. Brooke helped him. They worked in silence, circling the wagons and drawing up the stakes that held them steady. They untied the horses and harnessed them. They gathered the rocks from the fire pits. They were sweating as the wagons began to roll. They brought up the rear, trailing the third wagon, with two mules in tow.

"Is there money to be made in Wolf Creek?" said Brooke.

Marston shook his head.

"There's a life to live," he said. "Or that's what we hope. It's all we're after. I'd like to raise a family."

"It sounds easy enough," said Brooke. "What you're working on."

"Few things wind up actually being that way," said Marston, "but it's a straightforward plan."

"That it is," said Brooke.

Bird and Mary slept a good night's sleep with that family, their first in many. Bird slept outside. The man's daughter brought him furs and a few flints, sticks, and logs to make a fire. Mary slept inside, in a pile of furs. She did not bother to evenly distribute them upon the floor. She set them in a pile and worked her way into them. They sat heavily beneath and upon her.

In the morning, the man, whose name was Clark, brought them into town in a wagon he hitched to the back of his horse. His daughter brought up the rear, directing the ponies they were planning to sell that very day. Clark let Mary and Bird off the wagon near the center of town. Bird and Mary thanked them for their kindness and hospitality. Clark and his daughter were more than happy to help. They rode on to tend to business and left Bird and Mary standing together, but a few feet apart.

Town was busy, bustling, loud, and dirty. Men and women splashed through the mud, dashing from here to there. Shouts came from windows and doors swung mightily with the bodies of suited men and drunkards alike. In the very center of town there was a spiraling staircase. It curled up toward the sky and then stopped, as if there was a trapdoor at its top that might have led them from this world to the next.

"What is this?" said Bird, fingering the carving perched atop the banister at the bottom of the polished stairs.

"An eagle," said Mary.

"I know it's a bird," said Bird. "But why is it here?"

"I do not know," said Mary.

"I like this place," said Bird.

"It does not suit me," said Mary, holding the hem of her dress an inch or so above the mud.

"How can you know?"

"It's a feeling. The place is busy and loud. I preferred the ranch. I even preferred our building with a kitchen, on a good night."

"This place will do for now," said Bird. "There is money to be made here."

Two men fell out of a set of swinging doors to Bird's left. They were deep in a struggle, pounding one another with drunken swings. Mary startled, but was out of harm's way.

A crowd of men soon followed them from inside, keeping a distance but egging them on.

"He meant it," said one of the men. "Don't let him tell you otherwise."

"He's been saying as much for days now," said another.

They were laughing for the most part, making sport of these men.

Bird approached. He withdrew a pistol, but only to more laughter from the men.

"This broken boy has come to set you apart," said one of the men on the bar's stoop.

The two fighters paid no mind to any of it. One of the men was finally able to gain an upper hand. He was able to straddle the other man and pin him down. He pounded into his face and neck without discrimination. He was smiling. Bird announced himself with a shot, but neither of the men paid him any mind. A few of the men on the stoop whooped or yipped. It all seemed fairly ordinary. Mary withdrew. She did not like to see violence or feel the approach of violence, and this was too much of both.

She entered the building across from the bar, a post office that was seeing little action. A clerk sat behind the counter, busy with some writing. He lowered his pen to greet her, but Mary kept her back to him. Her gaze was at the window, in spite of herself.

"Which of these men is the richer man?" said Bird.

Neither of the brawlers took any notice. The one who had been straddling the other was losing his position. The other man had managed to get ahold of his throat and was drawing him steadily toward the mud.

"That would be him," said one of the men from the porch. He gestured to the man losing his grip, as the other rose up from the ground to gain control of the fight. "But I would stay out of it."

Bird approached the two fighters and stuck his pistol to the ear of the man who was now atop the other. The other man's face was pressed into the mud and he was struggling for air.

"Let him raise his head," said Bird.

The other man's hand came reluctantly from the back of his opponent's head.

"You, in the mud," said Bird. "Will you have me end this?"

The man in the mud nodded.

The other man eyed Bird at a slant.

"You will pay me five hundred for the task and provide a room for me and my wife."

The man in the mud nodded again.

The other man began to turn, but Bird fired and startled the street. Most of the men and women nearby flinched or ducked, and the man straddling the other man fell into the mud and did not move again.

Bird helped the other man up.

"I had him," explained the man. "You only expedited things."

"Yes sir," said Bird.

"It's only worth two hundred."

"That was not the arrangement."

"Two hundred and a bed and a bath for you and your wife," said the man.

"You've got a horse?" said Bird.

"A mule," said the man.

"I'll take the mule then," said Bird.

"I like a reasonable man. My name is Ramon."

"Bird," said Bird.

"Where is your wife?"

"Hiding in the post office."

Ramon glanced to the window and waved. Mary did not answer.

"Can I help you, miss?" said the postal clerk. Mary turned finally to explain that she was merely hiding there and there were no services needed.

"You're thinner than a rail," said the clerk.

"I have been on foot for some time," said Mary, "and eating little before it."

"I can get you a square meal for next to nothing," said the clerk.

"I have less than that," said Mary.

"On the house then," said the clerk. "My treat. We will eat and you can tell me how you wound up here. You can talk to my wife."

The postal clerk led Mary through the back of the post office and out a door that led into an alley. Across the alley was a small shack with smoke bellowing from its chimney. Inside, there was a table, two beds, three chairs, and a window. In front of the stove was a woman named Gretta. She was the clerk's wife. She had a heavy accent that made it hard for Mary to follow everything she said. But Gretta was very patient with Mary, and did not mind repeating herself.

"What is your name?" said Gretta.

"Isabella," said Mary.

"That is a pretty name," said Gretta.

"I like it very much, thank you," said Mary.

"Where is your family?" said Gretta.

"Pardon?" said Mary. She was slurping the stew they'd prepared: beef, potatoes, carrots, and peas.

"Your family," said Gretta. "Where are they?"

"Oh," said Mary. "I haven't got a family. I came here with a boy, but we are not related."

"Where is he?"

"He is finding work as a gunfighter, ma'am."

"Oh my," said Gretta.

"It is a foolish pursuit. He cannot shoot and has but one arm."

"He has something to prove then," said Gretta.

"You are correct," said Mary. "I'd like to talk about something else now. I've been with that boy for too long and I'm losing track of what it was I enjoyed besides."

"Where were you raised?"

"On a ranch some distance from here," said Mary.

"Where are your parents?"

"You're hounding the girl," said the clerk. "Let her eat."

"Father is dead and Mar— ...Mother is in the wilderness," she said.

"In the wild?" said Gretta.

"Pardon?"

"Where is your mother?" said Gretta.

"In the wilderness," said Mary.

"Why?"

"Gretta, please," said the man.

"She is hunting down a man who murdered half a town."

"Which town?"

"I do not know."

"Your mother is hunting down a killer?"

"She is very strong and brave," explained Mary.

"She must be a special woman," said Gretta.

"She is," said Mary.

"I'm finished," said the clerk.

"Then take your sleep," said Gretta. "I am talking with the girl."

"Why doesn't she like me?" said Ramon. He and Bird had made their way back into the bar and Ramon was ordering them drink after drink.

"Who?" said Bird.

"Your wife."

"She does not like many people," said Bird. "She's a contrary bull."

"Do you like working with a gun?" said Ramon.

"It's why I'm here," said Bird. "I would like to become a marshal, or a bounty hunter. I would like to head out and meet evil head on."

"A committed man," said Ramon.

Bird nodded.

"A dedicated man," said Ramon. "Here is to dedicated men."
He raised his glass.

Bird did as Ramon did. They drank, and Bird coughed. These
were his first tastes of liquor. He felt sick and then warm and
then sick.

"You are not a drinker," said Ramon.

Bird shook his head.

"But you are a gunfighter."

Bird nodded.

"A one-armed gunfighter," said Ramon.

Bird withdrew his pistol with a clap then set it back behind
his belt. One man startled, but the rest in the bar began to laugh.
Ramon clapped Bird on the back.

"Brave boy," said Ramon. "You are in the lion's den. But we
are friends. Here is your money."

He handed Bird a small pouch of coins.

"There is more than that too to be made," said Ramon. "We
like each other, no? You are getting to like me?"

Bird nodded. He opened the pouch and counted the silver. It
was two hundred even.

"Who was the man I killed?" he said.

"He was a bad man," said Ramon. "He was a killer and a
drunk."

Ramon ordered two more drinks and toasted to Bird again.

"To our newest hired gun," said Ramon. "You'll sleep with us
tonight. In the mission."

"Where is it?"

"At the end of the road. You cannot miss it. You will like it.
Your wife will like it. There is a bathhouse nearby, and you can
use it as you see fit."

"I did not expect this to come as easily as it has," said Bird.

"You were ready for it," said Ramon. He set his hand on Bird's bad shoulder, and Bird flinched but did not pull away.

"I am ready for it," said Bird.

"To fight evil," said Ramon.

"To face it head on," said Bird. "With everything within me."

"You are a very brave boy," said Ramon.

Bird found the postal office locked when he set to fetch Mary. He peeked in the windows and spotted nothing. He went around the side of the building and into the back alley. There, he spotted the shack and the smoke and approached the front door. He knocked and Gretta answered.

"Have you seen my wife?" said Bird.

"I have seen no wives," said Gretta. "It is late and you are drunk, boy."

"I can't find her," said Bird. "Her name is Mary."

"She has likely run away or is staying with her mother."

"What are you saying?" said Bird.

"She is likely with her mother," said Gretta again.

"She doesn't have a mother."

"Then you have yourself a problem, boy. Do you know what time it is?"

"I am not a boy," said Bird.

"You are no bigger than my gut," said Gretta.

"I am bigger than your gut," said Bird.

"You must go now," said Gretta. "My husband is sleeping and he will not be happy for you to wake him."

"But I cannot find my wife," said Bird.

"I know this," said Gretta. She shut the door.

Bird stumbled back into the alley. A cat darted past and vanished beneath a crate.

"That cat is like my wife," Bird said, to no one.

Ramon was waiting for him at the staircase. He was bent over, as if talking to the eagle.

"We have drunk, my friend," said Ramon.

"I'm sick," said Bird.

"You are not a drinker," said Ramon. "But you will get better."

"I do not trust you, Ramon," said Bird.

"Nor should you!" said Ramon.

Suddenly, Bird was laughing. Then Ramon was laughing. They were drunk in the street together and the stars were out. The windows around them were lit and dark and in-between. There was singing coming from the bar. Someone was banging out something on a loose-keyed piano. A man led his horse down the center of the road. Bird withdrew his pistol and stuck it back behind his belt.

"Come," said Ramon, "to the mission. We'll sleep now and get baths tomorrow. I'll introduce you to the boys and to the boss. I have a bottle in my room. We will drink before bed and in the morning to cure our stomachs and clear our heads."

"You are not the boss?" said Bird.

"I like you, little bird," said Ramon. "Do you like me just a little?"

Bird said nothing.

The mission was raucous, but clean. Men and women crowded the halls, and the enormous chapel space at its center. Corridors of rooms lined the edges and Ramon took Bird to his. It was sparsely decorated, but lined with empty bottles. They drank on the rug in the center of Ramon's room, and when Ramon began to touch him, Bird did not resist. Ramon removed Bird's shirt, and then his own. He touched the scar where the boy's arm had been.

"I was pinned beneath a rock," said Bird, "and I freed myself."

"You are a very brave boy," said Ramon. He kissed him then, and Bird retracted.

"No," said Bird.

"My mistake," said Ramon. "I thought you liked me."

"I will sleep outside," said Bird, and he gathered his shirt and dressed while exiting.

As he left the chapel, Ramon followed. The men and women in the hallways laughed at themselves and then at Ramon and Bird. They went back to laughing at themselves as Bird and Ramon left.

Outside, Bird found a fountain with a smooth bench carved into its outer wall. He set himself on the bench and told Ramon not to come any closer. He withdrew his pistol. When Ramon stopped, Bird set the pistol at his side.

"I will be fine here," said Bird.

"I can show you to your room," said Ramon. "I will leave you there."

"I will sleep outside," said Bird.

"You're upset," said Ramon. "I have upset you." He was distressed, but soft in his manner.

"I'd like a safe distance between us," said Bird. "You've made me feel uneasy, but I am not upset."

"I apologize, little bird," said Ramon. He was missing a tooth and the gap sometimes whistled as he spoke. "I did not mean to upset you."

"In the morning," said Bird, "you will introduce me to the boss?"

"Yes," said Ramon. "But you can sleep inside."

"I will sleep outside," said Bird. He pulled back the pistol's hammer and set it in his lap.

Ramon left him then. Bird sat alone. He set his hand in the

still water of the fountain. Mary had abandoned him. He would be alone forever. He was better off alone. He would be a traveler and a gunfighter. He would be quick and steady, and they would not expect it.

The bodies in Wolf Creek were arranged as if the townspeople had been executed in a group. The wagon train had sped in to greet the buildings, but now lingered at the mouth of the town's central road. They kept their distance, for fear of a plague, until Brooke volunteered to approach the corpses. He promised to remain at a good distance if he could not produce another viable cause of death. He approached the bodies with a bandana at his mouth, and yet the stench still struck him like a hand.

"They are shot," said Brooke. He coughed and retched from the smell. The sight was less than pleasant too, but nothing he had not seen before. "They are days dead. Maybe weeks."

Slowly, the wagon trainers approached.

"Who killed them, John?" said Irene.

"I do not know," he said.

"It's likely the same riders what killed the men in the stagecoach," said Jack.

"Or other riders altogether," said Marston.

Wendell fired his rifle in the air to announce their arrival.

"If anyone is still breathing in these walls, show yourself," he said. "We are not here for trouble. We've been traveling for endless days and we've come only to make a home. We will work. We will be good citizens of Wolf Creek."

There was no response. The wind howled through the hollow buildings. Wendell set the boys to gathering the bodies and burying them on the edge of town. He asked the women to go from door to door and check for life or supplies. He would go with them, for protection. He gave his young confidante a pistol, as well.

Working together, the men had the graves dug before sundown. They set the bodies one by one at the bottom of each, and filled in all the dirt.

They found the homes vacant. Some looked as if they had been lived in but abandoned with haste, others seemed to be packed away, as if the owners had had their fair share of life in Wolf Creek and had decided to seek fortune elsewhere. There was an endless turning over of property happening, explained Wendell. Some element of the life desired was always off and people were hunting down something quiet and peaceful, leaving their shells behind like the crabs he'd read about in books. Each of the wagon trainers had a theory to explain what had happened there. Most involved the sudden oncoming of some great misery. The homes that were packed away, Marston explained, likely belong to the people who were smart enough to avoid the snowfall, people who had some sense of what was coming. It had been almost unbearable that year, nearly everywhere. But the bodies he could not explain. Nor the unshakable feeling that the town had been caught by surprise in some way or another. There was blood all over the prison. Something tragic had occurred and had left the town full of bodies and ghosts.

There was little food to be found, but there was a well and plenty of beds and kitchens and lots of clothing. They butchered a mule and salted the meat. They set themselves up in the homes that were to their individual liking. Brooke asked his wife which home she most preferred and she looked at several before selecting one at the far end of town with a small fence at its side.

"For livestock," she said. "Horses or pigs."

Theirs was a small home on a small plot in a very small town. It had two beds, a couch, a fireplace and stove, and a large wooden dining table. For anything they needed, they scavenged. She found a piano in what was once the saloon and she had Brooke and Marston move it into their house. In what might have once been the inn, she opened an armoire in a back room.

"It's nice," said Brooke.

"But not for us," she answered.

The piano took up nearly a quarter of the shared space. She played beautifully. Brooke had never heard anything like it. It was not like bar music, or the upbeat steps you might hear in a brothel. She lingered the notes, let them ring out. She sang softly, songs he did not know. He kept his distance. She was growing confident in her confusion. She called him John and every time the smirk she wore softened. Soon, she called him John as if it were the name she'd always known him by. They lived together more as brother and sister than man and wife, but they had an affectionate air about them that gave their neighbors no question. Slowly, they began to cultivate the land that extended beyond their home. Brooke dug irrigation ditches and planted seeds he found in an abandoned shop near the center of town. They offered a percentage of their yield to Wendell in exchange for the first calf born from his livestock. Brooke also offered to work for him throughout the reconstruction of most of the buildings, or the destruction of those that were too far gone. They actively traded and dealt with the family, but they were less social here than they had been even while wagon training. Occasionally, Marston dropped by and spoke with Brooke. Marston was planning to open the store. He would get a line on products from the nearest city, an address for which he had discovered amongst the old mail that was clogging the cubby holes in the abandoned post office.

"It is as if we had stumbled into Paradise," said Marston.

They were seated in two of the four chairs claimed by Brooke and the woman he met in the snow, who had taken to calling herself Mary.

"And what if the good people of Wolf Creek return?" said Brooke.

"Wolf Creek is no more," said Marston, "for we are in Wendell's Valley."

They began to brew and grow and cattle were born. In not much time at all, each had fallen into step with a private life of sorts. Wendell and Irene occupied a home by the church, and led sermons and singalongs from the pulpit every Sunday. Marston, Jack, and Clay attended these weekly gatherings with the three younger women, Wendell's confidante, the slanted-speaker, and the girl who had been in the back of the wagon with Mary when she was ill. These women were named Clara, Dorothy, and Caroline, respectively. Clara, it turned out, was Marston's wife. Formally, at least. She seemed closer to his father, and achieved most of her ends by going through Wendell, rather than Marston. Caroline and Dorothy were sisters to Marston, Jack, and Clay, and Caroline was the youngest of the lot. They sat in the front pew together at the church, and every so often, Brooke and Mary would seat themselves in the back row to watch the proceedings, if only for the company.

They planted a sign at either end of the town, one facing the desert and the other facing the path that led in from the woods.

One night, Brooke and Mary were on the porch, just watching the sky. It was spectacularly plain. The clouds moved along at varying speeds. It was otherwise a constant shade of blue.

"Could you ever have imagined our lives would one day look like this?" said Brooke.

"I am not so sure what you imagine our life looks like," said Mary. "When I look, I hardly see anything at all."

They were quiet then. It was warm out. Mary had boiled the water for Brooke's bath, and it was cooling in the tub toward the back of the house. Their arms were still, perched on the rests their chairs provided. Flies worked a bit of manure just past the fence. A faint funnel of smoke lifted from the chimney of the cafe. A man came to town.

Bird did not sleep that night at the fountain. He slowly sobered and realized that he was cold and shivering. He warmed himself with his hand where he could. When the sun rose, he wandered back to the staircase and stood before it. He could not wrap his mind around it, and found it incredibly inspirational. It was beautifully crafted and solitary. It was hopeful and grand. He returned to the mission and found it quiet and still. He wandered the halls and saw no one. He left and walked to the adjacent building, in front of which stood a large man in a vest. It was a bathhouse, open to the public, explained the man. But it was not cheap.

"I am looking for the boss," said Bird.

"Are you looking for trouble?" said the man.

"No," said Bird. "I would like to offer my services as a gunfighter."

"You are a cripple," said the man.

"No, I am not," said Bird.

"You'll have to leave your gun at the desk," explained the man. He was smiling. Bird did not like the expression.

"I have killed one hundred men," said Bird. "I was in the army."

"You are a very brave boy," said the man.

"Do you know Ramon?" said Bird.

The man smiled. "I know him very well," he said. "I am his cousin. We work together. Do you... know Ramon?"

"We met last night," said Bird.

The man laughed then and said the boss would be more than happy to meet a friend of Ramon's.

The boss was a tiny man behind an enormous desk.

"You hope to be a gunfighter?" he said.

Bird was seated in a chair on the opposite side of the desk. The chair was appropriately enormous to match the desk before it. It seemed to swallow Bird as the boss's chair swallowed him.

"I am a gunfighter," said Bird. "I hope to find work. I have a wife and need a home."

"Our men live in the mission," said the boss. "Where is your wife?"

"I do not know," said Bird.

The boss smiled then.

"I see," he said. "You are friends with Ramon?"

Bird nodded.

"Ramon is a good man, and he is trouble." He had tiny eyes, the small boss behind the desk. They were focused, but there was nothing cruel in it.

A hand set upon Bird's good shoulder and he turned to meet the gaze of a considerable man in a top hat.

"Would you like a drink?" said the man. "You have the look of someone who has been out late with Ramon." He smiled.

"Yes," said Bird. "Something that does not sting, though."

"You are eyeing my hat," said the man.

Bird looked away.

"It's yours." The man placed the hat atop Bird's head.

"It suits you," said the boss. "Where were we?"

"I cannot honestly say," said Bird, fussing with the hat now. "I am not confident in my standing with you."

The boss laughed. "Nor should you be. If you come to work for me, you will only be as good as your last completed job. I do not carry much love for killers and fighters. I abhor violence and its necessity. Otherwise I would not need a mission of killers at my disposal. I am not so bad with a gun myself. Do you have terms?"

"I have taken two hundred per man, in the past," said Bird.

"Oh," smiled the boss. "Two hundred it is, then."

"And I want to know why you assign the targets you do," said Bird.

"You will not always like why. Sometimes, it is best not to know."

"I want to know. And I want the option to select who I go after. If you have a mission of killers at your disposal, each job will surely get done, regardless of my being the one you'd like to do it."

"You do not make a strong case for yourself as an individual," said the boss. "But I like a man with reasonable terms. And I like your new hat. And I like Ramon, though he is trouble."

"I would like only to pursue evil men, who have done considerable wrong," said Bird.

"There is no shortage of them, my friend," said the boss. He reached into a drawer at his knee and withdrew a stack of papers. "These are posters with deeds detailed. You'll see no man among them who does not deserve justice. In truth, the list is endless, the pages infinite, but these are the particular ones I have some personal interest in seeing brought to ruin."

Bird was quiet for some time. He leafed through the pages. He was soon met with his drink.

"The hat looks excellent," said the man who'd set the glass before him.

Bird drank. He turned page after page. The faces of these men and women were not so different, one to the next. Or their likenesses were poorly reproduced by a limited hand.

"These two men," he said, finally. He held up a deedless poster for two brothers, neither of whom wore a hat. "What is their full list of deeds, and what is your personal interest in them?"

"Those men are trouble," said the boss. "They are wanted in nearly every town for some reason or another, but they are not flashy or particularly skilled. Their crimes are many. Too many wrongs to list. A lifetime of wrongdoing. But they are not impressive enough for any kind of serious pursuit. They are not high profile. But, for me, it's a personal matter. They broke my man's nose." He gestured to the considerable man still perched behind them.

Upon closer inspection, Bird realized that he was, indeed, disfigured.

"They caused a ruckus in my bath. They brawled and drank and sought to wreck the peace. So I'll see them answer for their crimes. The news is that they have been apprehended, though. For a town they razed as mere boys. They were separated and brought to undisclosed locations. I have learned the whereabouts of one, though only through rumors in the street. This one," the boss put a finger to Sugar's likeness, "was set to bear a child. Left to their own devices, people will live out every possible variation of a human life. They are not at the top of my list, but if you can apprehend one or the other, I will pay you your two hundred. If that is where your interest lies."

"That is where my interest lies," said Bird. He examined the poster. Life was not at all what he expected, yet he was faced now with all he had ever known to hope for. "If they are already apprehended, is the case not cared for?"

"My man would like some time with them," said the boss. "What kind of boss would I be if I did not care for the desires of my men?"

"I would like to find them," said Bird.

"You seem excited," said the boss.

"I am ready, is all," said Bird.

They drank on it. He bathed. They clothed and armed him. They provided a holster and an uncracked belt. They provided a horse, which was fed and shod and roped to a post on the edge of town.

Bird found Ramon at the staircase, smoking.

"You are quick," said Ramon.

"There is work to do," said Bird.

"There is always more of that kind of work," said Ramon. "We did not expect to hold this place as long as we have. We have made a lot of enemies. Do you still like me just a little?"

"I like you, Ramon," said Bird.

"We are friends?"

"You are my first real friend," said Bird.

"Will you smoke with me?" said Ramon.

"Will you show me?" said Bird.

Ramon lit a cigar for Bird and told him to hold the smoke in his mouth, but not to take it into his lungs.

"You'll feel light-headed," said Ramon, "and then you will

216

feel a great charge. It is good for riding. The time passes more quickly."

"How long is the ride to Wolf Creek?"

"A day or two. You will find it pleasant."

"I had never killed a man before," said Bird. "Before we met in the street."

"I know," said Ramon.

"How?"

"You are eager in the way a killer is not. You are anxious too."

"Everybody likes you here, Ramon," said Bird.

"Really?"

"Knowing you got me in the door."

"That is nice to hear," said Ramon.

"Are you a killer, Ramon?"

"Yes," he said.

They were seated on the third step of the winding staircase. Ramon's knee tilted to meet with Bird's.

"Where did this come from?" said Bird. He took the cigar between his teeth and touched the beak of the wooden eagle.

"Someone carved it," said Ramon.

"But the stairs," said Bird.

Ramon shrugged. "Someone built them."

"But why are they here?" said Bird.

"They are nice to look at," said Ramon. "And no one tore them down." Ramon rose. "I cannot smoke a whole one of these in one sitting, and neither should you, little bird. Besides, you've got the day to ride and a man to catch. You had better get going, so you can hurry back."

"We could drink when I get back," said Bird.

"We will," said Ramon.

Bird rose, and they embraced. Ramon led him to the edge of

town, where the new horse was tied and waiting. He watched Bird remove the ropes and set the saddle. He waved to Ramon, who nodded back and turned away. Bird stubbed his cigar then, and lit out for territory.

Thanks, as always, to Andi—for everything. Thanks to Daniel Levin Becker and Eli Horowitz. Thanks to Charlotte Sheedy, Sam Lipsyte, Saeed Jones, Amelia Gray, Lindsay Hunter, Karolina Waclawiak, and Brian Evenson. Thanks to Dan McKinley and Jen Gann, for your horse sense. Thanks to Julie, Miles, Katie, Adam and the Mudds. Thanks to Eliza Wood-Obenauf and Eric Obenauf, and to everyone at Two Dollar Radio. Thanks to Ion, Claire, and everyone else at No Exit.

COYOTE

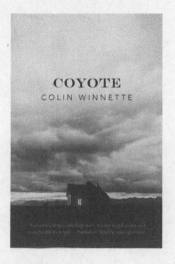

A daughter disappears in the middle of the night. What happens in the aftermath of this tragedy—after the search is abandoned, after the TV crews move on to cover the latest horrific incident—is the story of Coyote. There is a marriage and a detective. There is a storm, a talk show host, and a roasted boar. People are murdered and things are hidden. Coyotes skulk in the woods, a man stands by the fence, and a tale emerges within this familiar landscape of the violent unknown.

978-1-84344-842-6   £6.99

About Us

In addition to No Exit Press, Oldcastle Books has a number of other imprints, including Kamera Books, Creative Essentials, Pulp! The Classics, Pocket Essentials and High Stakes Publishing
> oldcastlebooks.com

For more information about Crime Books go to
> crimetime.co.uk

Check out the kamera film salon for independent, arthouse and world cinema > kamera.co.uk

For more information, media enquiries and review copies please
> contact marketing@oldcastlebooks.com